AN UNDYING LOVE

Though Christopher told himself such thoughts were simply the natural result of wishing to avoid wandering the country lanes of England alone and cold, stealing eggs and apples and pies from windowsills and never knowing who he really was, another thought tore at the frayed edges of his consciousness—the thought that if he left Alderley Village, he would never see Julie Williams again.

He couldn't help thinking of the future. If his memory never returned, he'd have to settle somewhere, take up some occupation, marry some lady or other. . . .

A liquid image of himself standing next to a woman and swearing undying love flowed sinuously into his mind. Like a man dying of thirst, he drank.

"Married," he murmured. What would that be like? A sudden ache of longing seized him, sharp and bitter. The image swirled, resolved. He felt dizzy. This time, the woman standing beside him was Julie Williams.

Ridiculous. He hardly knew her.

BOOK YOUR PLACE ON OUR WEBSITE AND MAKE THE READING CONNECTION!

We've created a customized website just for our very special readers, where you can get the inside scoop on everything that's going on with Zebra, Pinnacle and Kensington books.

When you come online, you'll have the exciting opportunity to:

- View covers of upcoming books

- Read sample chapters

- Learn about our future publishing schedule (listed by publication month *and author*)

- Find out when your favorite authors will be visiting a city near you

- Search for and order backlist books from our online catalog

- Check out author bios and background information

- Send e-mail to your favorite authors

- Meet the Kensington staff online

- Join us in weekly chats with authors, readers and other guests

- Get writing guidelines

- AND MUCH MORE!

Visit our website at
http://www.kensingtonbooks.com

THE
BLACKGUARD'S
BRIDE

Melynda Beth Skinner

ZEBRA BOOKS
Kensington Publishing Corp.
http://www.kensingtonbooks.com

ZEBRA BOOKS are published by

Kensington Publishing Corp.
850 Third Avenue
New York, NY 10022

All Kensington titles, imprints and distributed lines are
available at special quantity discounts for bulk purchases for
sales promotion, premiums, fund-raising, educational or
institutional use.

Special book excerpts or customized printings can also be
created to fit specific needs. For details, write or phone the
office of the Kensington Special Sales Manager: Kensington
Publishing Corp., 850 Third Avenue, New York, NY 10022.
Attn. Special Sales Department. Phone: 1-800-221-2647.

Zebra and the Z logo Reg. U.S. Pat. & TM Off.

First Printing: July 2003
10 9 8 7 6 5 4 3 2 1

Printed in the United States of America

For Julie Rain,
whose sweet mischief,
juicy laughter, intense hugs, and
clever mind make her mama smile
even on the most difficult of days.

ACKNOWLEDGMENTS

This is my fourth novel, and I'm still having a blast. I extend my sincere thanks to those who made this complex story easier to write: my mama, who looked after my little girls when the going got really rough and who loves my cliffhangers; my brother David Andrews and my invaluable critique partner Mary Louise Wells; my editor, Hilary Sares, who is generous with her time, expertise, and spirit; my agent, Jennifer Jackson, who cares; the wonderful readers whose letters I cherish; and my loving husband, Barry, and my dear daughters Julie Rain and Kathryn Rose, who listened and laughed and sniffled at all the right spots. Thank you, all.

Prologue

Gretna Green, Scotland
June 1817

It took every whisper of strength she possessed not to bolt from the courtyard of the makeshift chapel in a panic. He was waiting in there for her.

Calm . . . steady . . . one more step . . . calm . . . steady . . . one more step. She forced herself inside, keeping her gaze on the rough plank floor.

He reached for her hand, and she broke into a cold sweat. *Calm . . . steady.* She would only have to endure his touch for a moment. *Oh la,* she implored herself, *pray, do not retch!*

It wasn't supposed to happen like this, being wed. As a young girl, Julie Fitz had dreamt of her wedding day. She'd known just how it would be, right down to the last detail. The delicate gown and ethereal veil she would wear, the sweet flowers she would hold, the lavish decorations for the magnificent church, even the smart carriage her beloved would hand her into afterward. She'd be but seventeen.

Instead, here she was, a sad two-and-twenty, standing in a plain, ugly gray house in the tiny, shabby village of Gretna Green, dressed in her drab brown traveling gown. No veil. No flowers. And the smart carriage was now a hired coach—hers.

A few steps away, the door to a darkened room stood ajar. Countless couples, pursued by outraged relatives, had dashed in there to consummate their marriages. She could just see the foot of the bed, plain wood and plainer coverings. She shuddered and thanked God there was no one in pursuit, nothing to make a quick consummation of the marriage necessary, as it had been for so many other Gretna brides.

"Did you come here of your own free will and accord?" the parson asked.

She nodded. Oh, yes, the wedding had been her choice. She'd decided the lot. She'd chosen the day, the location, the ring, her clothing, and the mode of transport. The only thing she hadn't chosen was her groom.

The friend of a friend, Mrs. Ophelia Robertson—an outrageous and flamboyant old London hostess who knew everyone's business better than they did—had taken care of that. Dear Ophelia! She'd arranged the marriage, sparing Julie from dwelling on the details. Julie had never even seen the man she was to marry before today.

A tear of emotion—of which sort she was uncertain—welled in her eye and spilled over, not that it mattered. Her face was hidden from view by the heavy gray veil she had worn to block her view of her bridegroom. She hadn't thought she could bear seeing him standing there, waiting for her.

Feigning a need to clear her throat, she brought her hand to her face and dashed at another tear in frustration. La, there was no reason for her to be weeping, even if he was vile by all accounts. She needn't ever see him again after today.

She wouldn't see him *today,* either. A bark of hysterical laughter nearly escaped her. She beat it down with an effort and clutched at her reticule, where she'd tucked her spectacles before climbing down from her coach. For once, she was thankful for her extreme long-sightedness.

As the parson performed the ceremony, Julie responded woodenly, keeping her eyes fixed firmly on the floor. She did not wish to carry the memory of her husband's face or silhouette.

The vows finished, the blackguard she'd just promised to keep unto herself for as long as she lived placed the ring on her finger. The simple gold band glowed menacingly and burned, branding her with the symbolism of his ownership. Julie Fitz belonged to him now.

Thank God he did not want her. No man did.

Her fortune, however, was another matter.

Her position was loathsome and humiliating, but at least there weren't many there to witness the deed— only the parson, the Gretna innkeeper, and the parson's man-of-all-work, people she would never see again. The bridegroom hadn't brought along any of his friends or family—not that she was surprised. He didn't want a wife, he wanted money. There was no reason for either of them to announce their marriage.

Good.

Both of them would go on about their lives as before, though he would now have half of her inheritance to squander, while she would have the other half and so the means to live independently.

"You may now kiss the—," the parson began, but Julie was out the door and plowing headlong through the yellow summer sunshine toward her hired coach before he could finish the sentence.

"I say, are you not forgetting something?" her husband called out, emerging from the chapel house in her wake. The question brought her to a momentary halt, though she did not look back. A thrill of alarm clanged in her mind as she sorted through all the legalities of their bargain, but she was certain all was in order.

"Nothing is amiss," she said without turning around. "The papers have been duly signed and witnessed. As soon as you register the marriage in your home parish, my money will be waiting for you."

"Mine, you mean."

"Of course." Sensing his approach behind her, she shivered and hurried on to her coach. Waving to the driver to stay on his box, she climbed up with no assistance.

"In a hurry to leave?" her husband drawled, stepping up to the side of the hack. He hoisted himself onto the step and, leaning in through the window, flipped her veil back.

She was forced to look at him then, though without her spectacles, her view was quite out of focus. She had the fuzzy impression of short dark hair and a rounded face. "My business here is concluded," she said, trying not to squint. "There is no reason to linger."

"Ah, but m'dear, we have just been wed. It is customary to kiss. Hell, it is customary that I bed you." His brandy-laced breath washed over her as he leered. "Sure you want nothing more from me?"

"Sir, you know quite well I have no intention of sealing our bargain with a kiss—or anything else."

"I *am* your husband," he said, reaching out to finger the gold chain that hung about her neck, "and I could demand you comply." He skimmed the back of his cold fingers indolently across her bosom.

Julie's pulse leapt, and, though she forced herself

to be still, her voice shook with fear and anger as she said, "Yes . . . and I am your wife. And I could slit your throat as you sleep."

He tilted back his head and howled with unexpected laughter, and, though he was still hanging onto the side of the coach, Julie signaled to the driver to be off. The coach lurched forward, knocking her husband off balance. His eyes flashed indignantly as he righted himself, and before she knew it, he'd grasped her necklace and given the warm gold a savage tug. Pulling the severed chain and the locket that hung from it free of Julie's neck, he dropped to the black cobblestones below.

Her miniatures! She cried out, and her hand flew to her throat. The locket contained the only likenesses she possessed of her parents. They were dearer than dear.

Behind the coach, her husband laughed cruelly. "Something to remember you by, wife!" he called, his voice diminishing swiftly with the distance.

She thought about going back and attempting to take the necklace from him, but she knew it was impossible. He was too large, too muscular—and too foxed. She wouldn't put it past him to attempt to make good on his lewd suggestions. She shuddered and gave in to tears as she fumbled for her spectacles with shaking hands.

It would be three full days home to Alderley. She sagged back against the faded leather squabs and watched the landscape slide by, trying to put the locket from her mind. Gretna Green was a small village, little more than a few clay houses and the largish inn. Gretna was soon far behind, and there was nothing to occupy her mind but the dreadful thing she'd just done.

"Buck up, my girl," she said aloud. Talking to herself was a habit she'd picked up when she was small. From the age of seven, when her parents died of the same fever that stole her good eyesight, she'd led a lonely life in the care of her guardian, an uncle she'd never met before then, who had cared vastly more for her fortune than he had for her. He'd rarely paid her any attention at all. Isolated and lonely, she'd had no one else to talk to, and hearing her own voice had kept her from going mad.

She shook off the memory.

"The locket is gone forever, but you are free now. It is a time for exaltation, not sorrow," she admonished herself. "Allow nothing to ruin this day."

With one last sniffle, she dried her face and put the fuzzy image of the blackguard she'd wed aside.

She was free!

Her heart leapt with excitement and joy. For the first time since she was seven, she was free—free of worry, free to conduct her own affairs, free to live her life wherever and however she chose.

She would fade back into the country with her assumed name and half of her inheritance, back to the safe haven she'd found after running away five years before. Her new husband wouldn't be able to find her if he tried—not that he would—and he couldn't touch her money even if he did find her.

Not only that, but as soon as the marriage papers were registered in London and he laid claim to his half of her inheritance, her uncle would know her fortune was forever beyond his grasp, and he would have no reason to seek her out. He would forget her as easily as a man forgets his least favorite spaniel, and she would never see him again.

As the coach rolled south over the border into

England, Julie heaved a sigh. She was independent and safe.

She was also pragmatic by nature, and when her mind strayed from the lovely green countryside bathed in glorious afternoon sunlight and the scent of summer flowers to dwell on the locket once more, she told herself that if she had lost her heart's one treasure, she had only herself to blame.

"After all," she reminded herself, "you willingly married a blackguard, and you never expected to come away completely unscathed, did you?" Her only comfort was he couldn't know how much it hurt her to be parted from her necklace. The blackguard would probably derive great pleasure from her pain if he knew.

One

London, England
August 1818

The Viscount Whitemount was no one's friend, a policy that had served him well for all of his twenty-eight years, but he was forced to question its wisdom this night.

He had nothing.

He felt a drop of stray blood trickle over his cheek and splash onto his bare collarbone. He must look a sight—not that it mattered. Who did George have to impress besides the one-shilling whores and the Charlies?

He had no one. No family—or none who would receive him—and no friends either. It had been a shock to realize he had no friends.

"Not that I give a cur's last ballock anyway," he said with a sneer. Especially not now, when he was foxed to the rafters.

He grinned and then through the drunken haze wondered idly where he was going to sleep that night. Realizing it was probably close on sunrise anyway, he shuffled a little slower. He'd spent most of the last three days hovering near Jermyn Street, having lost the deed to his townhouse and his last guinea to that insufferable dandy, Pink Peplin, three nights before. He laughed at himself in derision. "It wasn't exactly *your* last guinea m'boy, but your boot-maker's or your chandler's," he muttered, finishing with a shouted, "may they rot in hell!"

He was at low tide and no mistake. "At point non plus. To the bad. Dished up. *Buggered and booked!*"

Somewhere in the darkness, a dog barked, but George's outburst went otherwise unheeded, and he walked on mindlessly, mostly because there was nothing else for him to do. If he sat down to sleep, he might be robbed again, and he didn't fancy the idea—not because he had much left to steal, but because the last band of thieves had kicked him savagely upon finding his pockets to let. He laughed drunkenly, remembering the first's expressions when the blood they'd realized they'd drawn with their beating had ruined his cravat and waistcoat.

"Clods." George spat.

The last bunch had taken the things anyway—*and* his fine linen shirt and his boots. The only thing they hadn't taken was his inexpressibles, and that only because the breeches were so tight they couldn't wrestle them off him. He gave a snort of laughter and then sobered a little. They'd taken almost everything.

Almost.

He patted the reassuring little cache at his hip. He had a secret pocket the thieves had missed. What he had there wasn't much, but it would buy him a tavern room for a night and breakfast in the morning.

And after that?

What *was* he going to do? He looked about him at the tall, tidy houses there on the tree-lined edges of Mayfair. Two years before, he'd have been welcome at any of those doors. Hell, he'd have been fawned over! Briefly, he thought of asking for shelter for the night, but before he could think of whose house to try, a carriage approached, emerging from the deep shadow like a barge on the River Styx, its shiny, black lacquered sides hardly visible until the equipage was well nigh on top of him.

As it approached, George recognized its lone occupant, a man dressed in formal black and white, Sir Edwin Parnley. They had never been close, of course, but two years ago they had been acquainted with each other well enough. Surely the man would feel compelled to stop and offer George some assistance, if he saw him.

For one terrible moment, George was torn between shrinking back behind a tree and calling attention to himself, between pride and need, but then, at the last moment, he called out and raised his hand.

Sir Edwin glanced his way . . . and then his gaze moved on, unkindled by even the weakest spark of recognition. The carriage rolled on, leaving George staring after it.

The baronet hadn't even recognized him.

George snorted. It wasn't the first time such a thing had happened. There was a time when everyone in the younger, faster set George ran in would have recognized him. Recognized him, hell! They would have come to blows to be seen standing next to him. He'd been powerful, at the pinnacle of society's regard, and he'd taken great delight in ruining those who would not fawn over him. But then he had snubbed the wrong person, the prince had given him the cut direct, the invitations had stopped flowing in, and things had changed.

One night he'd been denied entrance to Almack's. The week after that, it was Boodles and White's.

The gaming hells were all crooked, and his losses

had been heavy there. Six months after he'd been excluded from the gentlemen's clubs, he was so far up the River Tick that his valet—along with most of his other servants—had walked out on him.

He hadn't dressed himself in his life, and he hadn't any blunt or credit to stay in fashion anyway. The last straw was his hair. He usually wore a very dark, devilish fashionable Brutus style. Trouble was, it was a wig. His own hair was a less-than-fashionable mass of unruly blonde, and with no valet to keep it undetectably covered with the wig, his hair became a joke.

He stopped going out. For two months, he drank heavily instead of visiting the gambling hells and losing heavily, and when he finally worked up the courage to emerge—blond, poorly dressed, red-nosed, and having lost his paunch—almost no one recognized him.

Back inside he went, until desperate financial straits drove him forth three nights ago to gamble his last holdings in one desperate attempt to regain his life.

He'd lost.

Of course.

And now, here he was—unshaven, with long, unkempt sideburns, unwashed, unwigged, gaunt, and half-dressed. His own family would not recognize him. It was no wonder Sir Edwin didn't—and, hell, even if he had, the bloody craven probably wouldn't have stopped. George certainly wouldn't have stopped, were their situations reversed.

"What now?" he muttered.

Walk, his mind answered, as though hunger and the need of a bed had split his personality in twain.

"Where to?"

An inn, came the answer. *A cheap one.*

"Damnation. Used sheets, bedbugs, and worse."
In spite of his drunken state, George still had the
sensibility to shiver. It galled him to have to spend
his last copper in such a hellhole. This was his exit
scene. George DeMoray, the Viscount Whitemount,
should be going out with a defiant flourish, not a
tired moan.

As though he'd not suffered enough punishment,
the Heavens chose that moment to assail him. A few
heavy drops of rain fell, and then the leaden skies
opened up with a sudden, miserable torrent. His
breeches—once the finest any gentleman owned,
anywhere—slumped, a torn, sodden, and blood-
stained mass, the weight of them pulling at him, as
though trying to wrestle him to the ground, beaten.

Any normal man would have been flooded with
self-pity or shame or despair. Any normal man would
have fallen to his knees and begged for the Lord's intervention, but George DeMoray was no normal man.
Instead of admitting and embracing his own utter defeat, instead of begging for mercy, George lifted his
hand to the sky and clenched his fingers together
until his knuckles turned white.

Shaking his fist, he sneered with acid contempt
and gestured broadly about him. "God-all-blasted-
mighty!" he yelled to the Heavens. "Holy bloody
hell! What is this?" He spat into the puddle growing
about his feet. "Do you think you can punish me any
more than you already have? Go ahead, toss it down
then. A little rain cannot possibly make my life any
worse, you *bastard!*"

His words were still echoing off the cobbles when
his hair stood on end, and suddenly his skin felt as
though ants were stinging him all over. But he didn't

have time to react before a flash of sudden light blinded him, and a simultaneous roar filled his ears. He had a sensation of falling, and intense heat swam through his veins like angry fire, filling his ears, his eyes, his lungs, until he thought he would swell and burst. He felt his body slam against something hard, and intense pain exploded behind his eyes, as though his head had been split open like a coconut. He tried to lift his hands to his skull, but he found they were no longer his to command. They rose but then simply hovered, convulsing, masterless.

It was then that panic finally overtook him. It consumed him, even as his hand somehow found the secret pocket, and he clutched at the last pitiful leavings of his wealth.

White-hot, the metal seared his hand.

Clinging to reason, clinging to sanity, he felt himself fall once more, and then darkness found him. It stole over him, covered him in shadow, and his universe disappeared only to wink back into existence a moment later—except now it was wholly composed of a confused jumble of sensation and memory and dreams: he was a lad, running over a soft, green meadow, surrounded by dogs.

"Do not fret, my boy," a man soothed.

Who was it? His mind struggled to identify the familiar voice, but it was no use. The fog was too thick. Another memory possessed him, sharp enough to feel it: something wet pushing insistently at his hand. Pushing, snuffling, licking—dogs? He tried to move, but a ghost pushed him back down.

"Stay put, lad," the ghost said, "things have taken a nasty turn."

And then there was another voice, urging. "He's right enough. Best get on, sir."

He tried to focus but could not, though whether it was his mind or his eyes that would not obey his will, he didn't know. His head was pounding painfully, and he couldn't feel his body. Did he have one? Vaguely, he reasoned he must, for he could feel fur brushing against him and hear the whining of dogs.

Spirit dogs? Nonsense! There were no spirit dogs. And there were no spirit men, for that matter.

"Who are you?" he asked the voice, struggling to sit up, to free himself from the fog that sucked his mind downward into an impenetrable darkness, but then he stilled, for an even more pressing question had occurred to him.

"M'God," he slurred, "who'm I?"

For a moment, his eyes focused. A lined face resolved out of the fog, and the man repeated, "*Who'm I?* Bless me, my boy, do you not know?"

"I do not remember."

"What *do* you remember?"

He thought hard, his vision blurred, and his head ached. "Nothing," he answered, and then darkness closed over him once more.

Two

An unsigned note, delivered past midnight in London:

She was seen heading south on The Great Road in a coach and four in Northumberland three days ago. Find her.

All Julie wanted was sixteen hours of mind-numbing sleep, though she knew she'd have to settle for less than a third of that. It was past midnight as the coach pulled to a stop in front of Alderley Manor. The coachman was not a young man, and Julie had alighted by the time he could ease himself down from the box.

He took off his green woolen cap and hooked a bony thumb toward the interior of the coach, which resonated with loud, gravelly snores. "Sorry, miss. I guess the miles were too long for him."

She shook her head. "I daresay it was more the hour. You know Wells never makes it past nine o' the clock," she said with a charitable laugh, "even on Christmas."

But the coachman didn't share her amusement. "Yes, miss. I knew it right enough, and I oughtn't to have given him the job. It's my fault he's in there snoring and not riding lookout or even handing you down. A lady like you deserves better, and it's my job to see you have it. I ought to have brought a younger man."

Julie could tell by the poor man's tone of voice that his pride was hurt. "There is no younger man, save Sully," she said, "and he starts nodding earlier than Wells here." She chuckled. "It is not your fault if Lady Griselda will not hire new servants. Now, go see to the team and hie off to bed. You must be exhausted. We covered too many miles today."

In truth, they had covered fewer than thirty miles and that with four stops. But the two elderly men had both looked weary, and Julie had pleaded all manner of things from a megrim to gnawing hunger to make them stop and force them at intervals to rest.

The coachman smiled gratefully. "Well, I'd best wake Wells and—"

"Pray, do not disturb him," Julie said. "Why not just unhitch right here and let him sleep? He is curled up on the floor, so he cannot fall, and it is quite warm enough tonight. I shall send someone out with a pillow and blanket," she said, knowing full well she would be the one delivering them.

"Aye, miss," he agreed, fighting valiantly to stifle a yawn.

He began unhitching, and Julie turned to the house. As she'd expected, all was dark. The gray-haired footman on duty was softly snoring on the sofa in the front hall, and the lamp had gone out. After re-lighting it and delivering a pillow and blanket to Wells, she climbed the stairs, wearily rubbing the small of her back, but she didn't make it to the top of the first flight before a clattering commotion broke forth in the courtyard.

Wells!

She turned and fled back downstairs at a run, her heart and mind racing. What mischief could the old man have gotten into in that short amount of time? Flinging open the door and expecting to see God only knew what, she saw—

God only knew what.

A second coach stood in the drive behind the un-hitched first. The new arrival swayed and rocked from an apparent tumult inside, accompanied by whistling, yelping, whining, and barking.

Sir Basil.

Julie groaned. "What is Sir Basil doing here in the middle of the night?" For one insane second, she considered the merit of fleeing to her chamber and pretending she was already sound asleep. She'd had a long day. A long nine days, really, and Heaven knew she'd earned her bed. She looked skyward. "I deserve it, need it. It is calling to me."

But so did Duty. She sighed and squared her shoulders as Sir Basil's beefy coachman swung down and opened the coach's door, and a wagging, wiggling mass of dog and man tumbled forth. Sir Basil always traveled with his seven dogs—his "ladies," as he called them.

Named after the seven patronesses of Almack's, they were a noisy lot, most as irrepressibly cheerful in their barking as their master was in his speaking. The undisputed queen of the pack was first on the ground. She was named Lady Jersey, after the Almack's patroness known as "Silence" for her love of conversation, and the golden-haired mongrel was, predictably, the most vocal of the group.

Tiny, brown Lady Sefton was next, shy and biddable, like her namesake.

After that came Princess Esterhazy, a small, black bulldog mix who, while friendly, would nip unpredictably; and then Lady Cowper, who was a lovable and enthusiastic white poodle mix that looked more like a frisking lamb than a dog.

Two of the dogs, Lady Castlereigh and Mrs. Drummond-Burrell, "Dee-Bee" for short, were haughty and aloof spaniel sisters.

Last to emerge was Countess Lieven, a massive Russian wolfhound mix, who had the annoying habit of dancing lightly away when anyone but Sir Basil reached for her.

Unsettled as the ladies were to be traveling at so late an hour, they were especially noisy just then. Julie pushed up her spectacles and scowled. La, if she didn't do something quickly, they would awaken her mistress and everyone else at Alderley. That would be all Julie needed, an entire house full of ancient insomniacs! Seeing Sir Basil and his seven ladies settled for the night would be challenge enough.

The first order of business was quieting the dogs. Sprinting back into the house, she retrieved a plate of soup bones from the kitchen.

"One, two, three, four, five—oh la!—only six." Grabbing a hard roll for the loser, she scurried back out the door. "If I can just get the dogs settled, Sir Basil should be a—"

Her feet stilled as she came face-to-face with a half-naked stranger on the front steps.

Supported on one side by Mr. Biggs—Sir Basil's aptly named, very large coachman—the stranger wore no shoes, no coat, waistcoat, or shirt, nothing but extremely tight inexpressibles.

Julie's mouth dropped open, for she'd never seen

such a vast expanse of bare male skin in her life, not even when she'd helped Doctor Brown. Not that *that* would have made a difference, for there *were* no men in Alderley Manor like this stranger. None of the men at Alderley were so big or so muscular. A pair of massive shoulders gave way to a broad chest and a hillocky stomach. Is that how all young men were put together? She didn't know, but certainly they weren't all that tall. The man might even have been taller than Biggs, though she could not tell for sure, slumped over as he was.

And just how young was he? She couldn't tell that, either, for all she could see was the top of his dark blond head.

"Where do you want 'im?" Biggs asked.

"Hmm?" Julie started, realizing she'd been caught staring. "I—I beg your pardon?!"

"'E's 'eavy, miss.

"Oh . . . yes! Yes, of course. Put him down there." She motioned to one of the twin settees facing each other in the hall.

Lowered to the settee, the man's head lolled to one side in unconsciousness.

"He is bleeding!" Julie said. His dark straw-colored hair was matted with blood at the back of his head.

"*Was* bleeding," Sir Basil corrected, stepping through the door. "It stopped after a few minutes."

"Is he badly injured?"

"Do not fret, my dear. I think his wounds are not severe—though I fear my poor coach's squabs shall never recover! The fellow excels at bleeding."

"Head wounds are always that way," Julie murmured, bending for a closer look at the gash and immediately wrinkling her nose. The man reeked of spirits and smelled as though he hadn't had a bath in a month.

How odd.

His black breeches looked to be of fine cloth and cut. What sort of man wore expensive clothing but did not keep them—or himself—clean? She looked at him more closely. A pair of fashionably long but unkempt sideburns framed a face that might have been ugly or handsome. She could not tell in the darkness.

Julie looked over her shoulder and gestured toward her unexpected and unconscious guest. "Who is he?" she asked, dispensing with courtesy. After all, she could hardly expect a proper introduction to an unconscious man.

Sir Basil blinked. "I take it you do not recognize him?"

She shook her head and tugged at her short buff cotton gloves, which had begun to itch. "Don't you?"

Sir Basil hesitated a moment. "No," he said at last with a shrug. "I found him on the road, and I had hoped you might know who he was."

"I do not remember seeing him." *And I certainly could not have missed noticing a man like that one!* she thought, eyeing his massive shoulders. "Perhaps he lives beyond Buxley-on-Isis," she mused. "Perhaps Doctor Brown will know who he is."

Buxley-on-Isis, six miles down the road, was much larger than Alderley Village, and it had no doctor. Doctor Brown, who lived just down the lane from Alderley Manor, sometimes traveled that far to attend the sick.

"Perhaps," Sir Basil said, nodding.

"Or," she offered, "perhaps he is a guest at someone's house hereabout."

"An even more likely situation."

"I shall inquire in the village."

"Yes. Well. Whoever he is, he will be needing a warm bed as soon as may be, my dear. Oh, and those"—he nodded at the plate of bones she cradled in the crook of her arm—"do look . . . um . . . appetizing, my dear, but I dare say this poor devil might prefer something more . . . ah . . . restorative." He looked at his coachman and mouthed, "Strange gel." Then he addressed Julie. "Strong tea, perhaps? Coffee?"

The coachman, who was not the brightest candle in the sconce, looked uncertainly from Basil to Julie to the unconscious man and then down at the plate of bones and licked his lips.

"These," Julie quickly told him, barely suppressing a laugh, "are for the dogs. When you have them settled, there is a meal for you in the kitchen—pork pie and cold chicken. Do not drink all of the milk. My mistress requires a measure for her morning chocolate." The coachman didn't wait but took the plate and disappeared out the front door, the dogs following the plate of bones with single-minded attention.

"And you, Sir Basil," she said while nudging the footman-on-duty awake, "look weary. A room is prepared for you."

"Not the one with the view of the pond. I cannot abide—"

"Cannot abide the sight of water in the morning. Yes, I know, Sir Basil. Do not fret. You shall have the room on the northeast corner, same as last time," she said. *Same as every time.* Sir Basil was a frequent visitor to Alderley Manor.

"Pinkley, pray show Sir Basil to his chamber," she told the groggy, blinking footman and lit a candle.

"Yes, miss." The sleepy man tugged his gray fore-lock.

"Oh, but my ladies—" Sir Basil protested.

"Will be taken care of," Julie said.

"Oh, but you know they do not like sleeping in the stable yard. Lady Jersey cannot sleep on any-thing harder than down, and Princess Esterhazy—"

"Is allergic to alfalfa. Yes, yes," Julie said, patting his hand, "I remember well, Sir Basil. Not to fret. I know all of their particulars, of course. I shall have your coachman bring the ladies up to join you when they have eaten and . . . er . . . taken a stroll."

"Oh! Splendid. Then I should like to be shown to my bedchamber, if you please," Sir Basil said, as though the idea hadn't occurred to Julie yet.

"Indeed." She smiled and carefully handed Pink-ley the candlestick. "Mind your step," she called after them. She was unsure which of the two men was older. They both had to be in their seventies. When their footsteps had receded up the stairs along with the lamplight, she turned to the uncon-scious man on the settee.

"And now you," she said, knitting her brows. "What in the world am I to do about you?"

It was plain that the man was ten sheets to the wind and foundering on the rocks, but she worried he was truly injured in spite of Sir Basil's assurances to the contrary. "You certainly took a nasty blow to the face. Or two," she said, holding the light closer and peering at the man's swollen features. His torso, too, was bruised in several places. It appeared as though he had either been fighting or taken a nasty fall.

"Possible internal injuries," she said. "I had better fetch the doctor."

Pulling her cloak from a peg near the door, she hurried outside and down the drive. The doctor's cottage was just down the lane.

Doctor Brown was a taciturn young man, and Julie dreaded to wake him. He was always exceedingly cross when disturbed at night, and every time she did it, he rang a peal over her. But his gruff exterior concealed a kind soul. His eyes were caring and quick, and his hands were gentle, but competent.

A largish portion of Lady Griselda's household budget went to see he was well situated, and in spite of his frequent trips to Alderley at night, he wasn't about to seek greener pastures. He had come to love the inhabitants of Alderley Manor— which people in these parts jokingly referred to as Elderly Manner—as much as Julie did. Which was why she well nigh laughed at his scowl when he came to the door.

His housekeeper had long ago stopped answering the door at night. It was always the doctor who was wanted, and what was the use of two of them being awakened? He wore a heavy yellow cotton banyan and carried his medicine bag.

"Who is it this time?" He growled. "Wells? Darling?"

"Neither," Julie said. "It is a young man this time, a traveler. He arrived with Sir Basil and is unconscious. I think he is simply foxed out of his mind, but it does appear as though he has suffered some blows, and there is blood—"

"*Blood?*" The good doctor didn't wait to hear

more but surged down the lane, leaving Julie to scurry along after him.

It was a long night.

With no one else to assist him, the physician kept Julie busy for a time, fetching this and that. She grumbled her way along Alderley's darkened passageways, her aching body resenting every weary step. The man was nothing but another one of Sir Basil's strays. Plainly, he'd fallen into some misfortune, but Julie couldn't find much sympathy in her heart. There wasn't much blood, not enough to be life-threatening, and the mongrel likely had it coming to him. He looked—and smelled—a disreputable sort to her.

What else could he be, half dressed and foxed as he was?

As Julie stepped in with another warm blanket and a roll of lint, she kept her eyes firmly fixed upon the wall opposite the bed and placed the things on the dressing table.

The doctor noticed. "His modesty is preserved to a nicety with the counterpane. Hand me that blanket."

Julie did so and then helped the doctor spread the blanket over the stranger.

"Your diagnosis?" Doctor Brown asked. It was a game he liked to play with her.

"Well now, he is intoxicated for a start."

"And . . ."

"And in shock."

"Symptoms?"

"Shallow breathing, sweating, a little white at the fingernails. Not a severe case, but there, just the same."

"Anything else?"

"Possible internal injuries, though that grows less and less likely." He was sleeping comfortably with no sign of serious injury.

"Mmm." Doctor Brown nodded. "Treatment?"

"Keep him in bed and calm—no challenge there." She gave a wry grin. "Take off his damp clothing, which you have already done, I see," she said gesturing toward the untidy wad of cut-up breeches on the chair. "Keep him covered but not over-warm. Basilicum for those scrapes on his face and torso. No spirits or anything else for a time."

Doctor Brown nodded his head of straight black hair and gave her a rare smile. "Well done, Miss Williams!"

Inwardly, Julie flinched at the use of the false surname, as she always did when someone was being especially kind to her. The lie was necessary—but that didn't make it seem any less deceitful, and the doctor certainly wasn't someone untrustworthy. She'd been tempted to tell him the truth, that her real name was not Williams, many times, but something always held her back.

Of all the people who were a part of her new life since her escape, only Ophelia Robertson knew the whole truth about Julie's past. Lady Griselda and Sir Basil knew her real name, but they did not know of her clandestine marriage.

"You are learning," the physician said. "Aside from missing the burns on him—"

"*What burns?*"

The doctor grinned. "Then you truly did miss them, hmm? You are not just toying with me?"

She narrowed her eyes at him. "Are *you* toying with *me?*"

"Miss Williams. I am many things, as you yourself have, at various times, informed me: irritable, stubborn, and unreasonable. But I am not stupid. I will own as I have a thousand times before that you possess a natural aptitude for this sort of work—"

"You are forgiven." She smiled.

"—and that you might have made a fine physician, had you not had the misfortune to be born female."

"It is quite unfair," she said, allowing a bitter note to climb into her voice.

"Indeed," Doctor Brown agreed patiently. The two of them had shared the same exchange many times. She often assisted him as he tended the sick.

At first, she'd done it out of necessity; as the youngest person in residence by a margin of at least forty years, Julie was often the only one awake when the doctor arrived. Though it was sometimes exhausting work and always worrisome, she'd discovered a most unladylike interest in it, along with an aptitude the doctor recognized and praised right away.

"I will never understand," she muttered, more for her own benefit than for the doctor's, "why the profession is not considered suitable for ladies. Our sensibilities are not as fragile as they are accused of being. After all, is it not the women who endure pain, disfigurement, and blood loss to give birth? Do we not willingly, even joyfully, endure the stretching and tearing? And then do we not nurse the babies? Sop up soured milk? Bandage scraped knees, catch vomit—or not—and keep vigil night after night through the lot of our children's illnesses?

"And then there are the diapers—la! They are enough to make the Duke of Wellington blench and turn away, and yet we, 'the weaker sex,' face them down all the time without blinking.

"I daresay there is nothing more ladylike than tending to a dependent's physical needs. Why is it that as soon as a child reaches a certain age it is suddenly 'unladylike' to care for them? It is not logical. It is not fair. It is waste of human potential. It is—"

She looked up at the doctor, who was waiting patiently for her tirade to end, amusement dancing about his face.

"Oh, dear." She rolled her eyes. "Do pardon me."

The doctor shrugged. "No need. I share your frustration, after all, your belief in the inherent capability of women—elsewise, Lady Griselda would never have given me this position."

He grasped the patient's wrist, checking his pulse. "I truly do believe ladies will be allowed admittance to the medical schools in time."

"Not *in time* for me to attend them." Julie thumped the bedpost. "*I* shall have to be content to help you tend those here at Alderley."

"A formidable enough task," he said with a grin.

"Indeed." Julie chuckled in spite of her irritation. "How is his pulse?"

"Still too rapid for my liking, but slowing and strengthening, I think. Here, there are more wounds to be dressed." The doctor flipped back the covers to reveal the man's right hand and foot, which each bore a round spot an inch or so wide, blistered and blackened.

"Are those burns?" Julie asked.

The doctor nodded. "Curious, are they not?"

"Mmm, yes," Julie agreed, assisting the doctor at cleaning and bandaging the wounds, "they do look odd. Not at all like the water scald on Cook's wrist nor the fire blisters Wells suffered last month. They almost look like mud."

"Even I," the doctor said with a grin, "the greatest physician who ever lived, misdiagnosed them. For a second or two," he added with a jaunty flourish.

She threw him a speaking look, and he laughed.

"Now that we have established your preeminent knowledge and supremacy over me—"

"My complete and utter supremacy," he said.

"Do not tempt fate. Remember, if you become ill, I am the only physician you are likely to have for at least two hours."

He held up his palms. "I yield and confess that, upon first glance, even I overlooked the burns. I thought they were mud caked onto those spots."

"Are you sure they are burns?" she asked.

"Nothing else could do this, but they are of a curious nature."

"And in a curious location," she said. "I can understand the burn on his hand, but on the bottom of one foot? How in God's name could he—"

"Lightning," Sir Basil said in the doorway. "The poor man was struck by lightning. Saw it happen myself." He was dressed in nightcap and gown, covered with a banyan much like the doctor's but for being fashioned of blue damask.

"Sir Basil," Julie said. "You should be in bed, sir."

"Could not sleep. Worried about our guest, here."

"But, sir, the night vapors are not good for your—"

"Nonsense," the old man said, not unkindly. "*I* am not the invalid, *he* is." He pointed to the man in the bed. Doctor Brown was just finishing the last wrapping. "How is he?"

"He will live," the doctor pronounced cheerfully, "though I suspect he will wish he had not. Between being struck by lightning and being foxed—"

"And robbed and beaten," Sir Basil added.

"Oh?"

"Yes, saw that, too, though I arrived too late to stop it. Probably would have been much worse had I not happened along and scared the devils away. Five of them."

Julie had to turn her head to one side to hide her smile. The doctor, for his part, suffered a sudden, suspicious fit of coughing. With his slight frame and white hair, Sir Basil was hardly one to inspire fear in a gang of ruffians. It had to have been the appearance of Mr. Biggs that set the attackers to the retreat.

"A beating and then a lightning strike?" Doctor Brown managed at last. "It is a wonder he is still alive. Lucky man."

"Lucky?" Sir Basil muttered. "We shall see."

"What do you mean by that?" Julie asked, thinking she had detected a note of something . . . odd in Sir Basil's voice.

"Hm? Oh! Nothing, my dear." He yawned.

"You should seek your bed and some rest, Sir Basil," Doctor Brown advised. "No need to worry about our friend here. I vow he shall be right enough in the morning—all but for an aching head."

"He is not recognizable," Sir Basil whispered. He was most uncomfortable standing in Griselda's bedchamber in the middle of the night. His intentions toward her were honorable. They always had been.

Coming to her like this at night was risky, but it could not be helped.

"Did you tell Doctor Brown or Miss Williams who he is?" she asked, her white hair, falling in silky waves over her shoulders, as beautiful now as it had been in her youth. Sir Basil had always wondered what it would be like to touch her hair. Would it feel as silky as it looked?

"Sir Basil?"

"Hmm!" His eyes snapped to attention.

"What did you tell them?" she repeated.

"Ah. Nothing, nothing at all. I propose we tell no one. His appearance is quite changed, you see. I daresay you would not recognize him—no one would, save me. Not that any of us—me, you,"—he grimaced—"nor anyone else you are likely to invite here—run in his circle anyway."

"Former circle, you mean."

"Quite so," he said.

Griselda shook her head. "I have invited Ophelia Robertson. She is to act as my chaperone. Her circle is quite . . . broad. She knows everyone, and she is shrewd. It would not surprise me if *she* recognizes Whitemount when no one else does."

"It would surprise me," Basil said. "You have not seen him, dear lady. Nevertheless, it would be a disaster if she were to recognize him and say so in company. I think you had better tell Mrs. Robertson he is the Viscount Whitemount, just in case. And swear her to secrecy. With any luck, no one else will recognize him. He can stay here, and no one, including him, need know who he is. If the poor boy has lost his memory, well then, good for him, I say."

Lady Griselda pulled her wrapper more tightly

around her and considered for a moment, staring into the fire.

"I think you have made the right decision, Sir Basil. I will help in any way I can."

"I knew you would," he said.

Three

Reply to note:

Sunrise. Leaving this hour. If your bitch was on the North Road three days ago, we will find her. Be ready.

The cocks had all stopped crowing by the time the infernal doctor made a move to leave. The patient, for his part, was blasted tired of being poked and prodded. His head was splitting open, he was wearing an ill-fitting yellow cotton banyan—which was all he wore, to his discomfiture—and the doctor refused to give him what he really needed: a hefty draft of brandy. But the worst insult was the window. The doctor had pulled back the draperies and swung open the window, admitting a most foul fresh air and an even more scurrilous sunshine.

"If you were any sort of real doctor, you would do something about the light stabbing my eyes."

The doctor packed up his bag and rang the bell. "And if you were any sort of patient, you would allow the doctor to determine what is best for you. Fresh air and bright light will do you good."

He had awakened an hour before, and it seemed to him the physician had done his best to make him as uncomfortable as possible for most of that hour.

"Are you right and tight I did not have a pair of spectacles on last night?"

"Not only am I certain you were not wearing any last night," the doctor said, peering closely at his face, "but I am also quite certain you never wear them at all. Elsewise, you would sport the usual indentations. Since you have none, I can conclude either that blurry vision is new to you or that you are a vain, bang-up popinjay who refuses to wear spectacles."

"Perhaps it is the light that is making my vision blurry."

"Perhaps it is the light*ning* that made your vision blurry. You cannot expect to be struck so and come away unscathed. You may count yourself lucky that two burns and blurred vision are all you suffered. You are fortunate to be alive, Mr. . . . ?" The doctor peered at him hopefully.

Seconds ticked by as his mind worked furiously. "Nothing," he said.

"Ah well. . . it was worth a try. It is said that experiencing familiar situations or events can trigger the return of memories in cases such as yours. I thought the simple act of having to introduce oneself might—"

A young woman stepped inside the bedchamber. She was small and pale, with golden brown hair, and she moved quickly, as though she were used to hurrying. "How is he, Doctor Brown?"

"He will live," the doctor pronounced cheerfully.

The young lady turned to him. "How are you feeling, sir?"

"My head has split open, but my body does not have the good grace to turn up its toes."

Doctor Brown chuckled and closed his bag. "Perhaps the memory of your aching head will serve as a reminder not to imbibe to excess."

"Undoubtedly," he answered, "as there are no other memories to compete with it."

A squeaking noise escaped the young woman hovering near the door, and she looked to the doctor. "No other memories?"

The tired physician sagged against the bedpost. "It appears your houseguest has lost his memory," he said. "His entire past is gone."

"La!"

"Not to worry, Miss Williams," Doctor Brown replied. "As I have explained to our patient here, I have read of cases such as this, and in most of them the patient's memory returned within a fortnight or two. Sometimes, the lot comes back at once, and in others it returns in dribs and drabs. And it does not all disappear uniformly, either. Why, I read of one poor woman from Salisbury who did not recognize her own children. She knew she had a boy and a girl, and she knew their names, but she did not know them when she saw them."

"Speaking of names," the patient began, "I do not seem to remember mine."

The doctor frowned. "Mmm . . . yes. Devilish awkward, that. Perhaps you should choose one to use temporarily."

"Yes. Yes, I suppose you are right. But what name should I take? Suppose I never recover my memory? I could be stuck with whatever name I choose for a very long time. Maybe forever more. I do not know . . . 'Robert'?" he mused. "Or . . . 'Michael'? And should I choose a surname?"

Doctor Brown waved a hand. "Not my area of expertise. Leaving. I am for bed." He stifled a yawn.

"Perhaps Miss Williams here will help you choose—after she carries up some breakfast. Nothing too heavy," he told the young woman. "Weak tea. Toast."

"Of course," the young lady murmured and left. As she went through the door, she turned slightly to the side and her bare arm brushed her gown, straining the fabric against a shapely thigh.

The doctor caught him staring and raised one eyebrow. "No strenuous activity. At least not for a few days."

"Who is she?" he asked, not even attempting to pretend he'd felt no spark of interest. While her face had been a blur, he could see she possessed a fine figure and a luxuriant mass of glossy, golden-brown hair.

"Miss Julie Williams is her name."

"A housekeeper?"

"Not exactly," the doctor replied.

"A maid?"

"Her position defies description," Doctor Brown said. "I believe she is properly styled as Lady Griselda's companion, but in reality her duties fall far beyond that." He yawned. "I shall send several pairs of spectacles up as soon as may be. Choose the one that works the best and send the rest back to me."

"How much do I owe you?" he asked.

The doctor laughed. "Unless you have something hidden on your person, you have nothing to pay me with." He scooped up a shredded rag that might once have been a pair of disheveled-looking inexpressibles from the chair at the dressing table. "These are all you were wearing when you were brought here. Evidently, you have nothing else."

"No papers, no coin, nothing," he murmured, "and still you tended me?"

The physician shrugged. "As you are a guest at

Alderley, my fee is already covered—though I thank you for thinking of it."

His patient scowled. *What the devil?* A physician thanking him? *For what?* He hadn't been thinking of the doctor, he'd been thinking of himself. Doctors always expected their patients to pay on the nail. Didn't they?

The tired-looking man turned to go. "Oh." He stopped. "You may rise after you have supped, if you feel up to it, but remember, no strenuous activity." He grinned. "Not that she would allow it anyway." He strode out the door, muttering, "God knows I have tried."

He sighed and settled back into the pillows, looking about the chamber. Neither luxurious nor Spartan, the room was adequately appointed with a wardrobe, a dressing table, the four-poster, and a pair of chairs flanking a window that was, disgustingly, still open. He squinted at the morning sunlight slanting through the opening. The beams bounced off the too-bright yellow walls and polished wood floor, raising a riot of light-pains in his head. He groaned and, throwing the covers back, swung his bare legs out over the edge of the bed. The moment his bandaged foot touched the floor, it felt as though it were on fire, but he endured the pain and walked to the window, galled to find he was unsteady as he did so. Reaching the window, he raised his bandaged hand to close it and the draperies, but a glance outside gave him pause.

Nothing looked familiar.

A wave of dizziness overtook him, and he clutched at the sill to steady himself even as his eyes roved over the vista outside.

Apparently, his vision was only afflicted when looking at things nearby, for, while everything in the room was blurry, if he looked across the green lawn, he could clearly see it sloping down into a wide park with a brook that became a glassy pond at the edge of a forest. "I have never been here," he said. "Or have I?"

He just didn't know.

His eyes took in the scene, grasping for something familiar and latching onto a small pavilion fashioned after a Grecian temple. *A Grecian temple. Grecian. Greek.* "Alpha, beta, gamma, delta, epsilon . . ." he murmured. "I know Greek!"

"Who am I? *Quis sum ego?* By Jove, whoever I am, I know Latin, too." He was an educated man. A scholar of some sort. Was he a vicar? The son of a wealthy man who had attended school with other sons of wealthy men? Or was he a poor man with more curiosity than prospects?

A sense of emptiness stole through him, but it did not frighten him. Instead he felt . . . "Relieved," he said aloud. "Relieved and calm." *How odd.* He should have been feeling uneasy, disoriented, shouldn't he? But he didn't. It was almost as though a weight had been taken from him. He felt light and . . . and happy, almost.

As he stared at the temple below, a sudden vision assailed him. Another row of Grecian columns, these with greenery entwined among them. Christmas greenery? Was he remembering a Christmas celebration? People often decorated with boughs and vines at Christmastime.

"And how do I know that, if I cannot even remember my own name?" he said. His eyes found the columns outside again. He could almost feel them tickling his memory. "Christmas," he murmured, "Christmas. . . ."

"Well," the companion's voice chirped behind him, "I see we have one thing in common, you and I. We both converse with ourselves."

He turned. She bore a breakfast tray. He couldn't see what was on it, as it was covered with a green cloth, but he didn't care. He was suddenly ravenous, and his mouth watered. He would eat anything she'd brought.

The young woman wore a pleasant expression, but he knew that could not last long. This place belonged to one of the wealthy gentry, if not someone of the *ton,* and he was . . . a burden. If he didn't remember who he was in a hurry, that pleasant expression of hers would fade, and he'd find himself out on his arse and sleeping in a haystack.

She was staring at him, waiting for a reply.

He didn't know what to say.

"Oh! I am sorry," she said. "How clumsy of me! We have not been properly introduced. I am Miss Julie Williams." She curtseyed.

In spite of his intense hunger, he made an attempt at politeness. He bowed low—too low, for once more he had to clutch at the windowsill to preserve his balance. She moved to assist him, which nicked his pride, and he held up one palm to stop her and straightened.

"I am . . . that is, you may call me . . . Chris," he blurted, latching onto the first name that came into his head. Obviously, he'd mined his thoughts of a moment ago for the name. *Christmas . . . Chris . . .* it was as good a name as any, and—hell and blast!—for all he knew, it really *was* his name.

"It would hardly be proper for me to call you by your first name," she said. "We have barely met. You hardly know me."

"I know no one at all, not even a little," he said, "and I daresay that after last night you know me much better than many young ladies of my acquaintance."

As soon as those words had escaped, he wondered what had possessed him. Miss Williams, by the look of her, must have been wondering the same thing. Her eyes widened, and, even through the blur, he could see her blush a brilliant shade of pink.

Watch your step, Chris old man, or you shall find yourself tossed out on your arse sooner than you expect.

He put his hand to his head. "The lightning must have curdled my brain. Forgive me. What I meant to say was Doctor Brown informed me you assisted him in dressing my wounds—"

"Yes, w—well . . . ," she stammered.

"I mean no disrespect," he said quickly. "I am only trying—very clumsily—to thank you and to say I am ashamed I could not properly comport myself last night. Apparently, I was . . . well, foxed." He prepared himself for the censure he knew was coming, but it never arrived.

"You were," she agreed.

He thought he heard laughter lurking in her rich, melodious voice. If he hadn't known from the start she was his adversary, he might have decided he liked that voice. But she, judging from what the doctor had said, held enormous sway around this place, and she might just have the power to either keep him around or to send him packing. With no blunt and no memory, he was in a predicament, and no mistake. He would bend all of his attention toward turning her up sweet before she turned him out of the house—and he might as well start by parrying her laughter— which he rather suspected was born more of sheer mockery than of friendly amusement. He knew—without knowing how he had learned such a cruel lesson—that ignoring mockery would not make it go away. He was possessed of the sure knowledge that the best way to parry such a blow was to openly deplore himself to the point of ridiculousness.

"For my condition last evening," he said, "I truly do apologize. Whatever else I am, I am certainly an utterly irresponsible knave without benefit of wit or restraint, and I humbly prostrate myself in supplication of your mercy and forgiveness."

She laughed, as he hoped she would. "I forgive you. Now, back in that bed, honey-tongued knave! You should not be up."

"The doctor authorized me to rise as soon as I felt ready," he said.

"My eyes tell me you do not feel ready."

He grimaced. "Your eyes do not lie. Unfortunately."

"Come," she said, and, setting down the tray, she looped her arm through his and guided him back to the bed.

"I need your steadiness more than my dignity would wish," he said.

"Dignity does not belong in a sick room," she responded.

"A man is nothing without his dignity. You may trust my opinion on that, for I am an expert. Dignity—and one very soiled pair of cut-up breeches—is all I have. That and a false name."

"So," she said, obviously refusing to dwell on the more unpleasant aspects of his peculiar situation, "what shall I call you, Mr. . . ?"

"How about Chris?"

She gave him a sidelong glance.

"Christopher?" he coaxed.

"It would not be proper."

Though he couldn't see her clearly, he could *hear* the wrinkled-nose tone in her voice, but he could also sense the underlying good humor and desire to be friendly. She would capitulate, if only he persisted. Again, he didn't know how he could know that with such certainty, but know it he did. He seemed to be adept with people.

"Ah," he said with a shake of his head, "but if I choose no surname, then you shall be *forced* to call me Christopher."

She shook her tilted head. "Yes. I suppose I shall."

"Then I am simply Christopher. Chris to my friends," he added, grinning.

"Well . . . I suppose there is no one here at Alderley who would raise an eyebrow at hearing me utter your given name." She tilted her head even more and laughed. "Truth to tell, there are few here at Alderley who can hear me utter anything at all."

"Is this some sort of asylum for the deaf?" he asked.

"Oh, no indeed." She laughed. "Alderley Manor is a private residence, the home of my mistress, Lady Griselda Warring."

"Then why is it populated by the deaf?"

She laughed again. It was a sound that came naturally to her, spilling forth as freely as water over a fall. She was obviously a happy person. For some reason, the thought annoyed him.

She gestured about her. "All of her ladyship's servants and retainers are at least as old as she is."

"I take it she is past the first blush?" he asked.

She dimpled. "Well past—though I do still see her blush from time to time. She is a dear person. Always happy, always kind."

"Come now," he said with a skeptical wave of one hand. "Surely not always."

"Only wait until you meet her. Everyone loves her as dearly as I do. You will be no exception."

"In that case, I look forward to being quite ordinary." He threw her a disarming smile. "Now, back to the servants—surely not all of them are so aged."

She nodded. "All of them. Lady Griselda will not consent to the hiring of new servants. She simply cannot bear to risk making anyone feel obsolete or unwanted. Most of them have been here since she first came here."

"How long ago was that?"

"It must be . . . oh, forty years, or more."

"All of her servants have been here that long?" he cried.

"Yes. Well. . . most of them. A few have been here even longer. She treats them more like family than servants, and they are all fiercely loyal to her. They will not leave her service."

"But what about the field hands? The plowing, reaping, threshing, shearing . . . those are not tasks for old men."

She pushed up her spectacles. "The Alderley flock was given into the care of the villagers some years before I came here. The fields and orchards likewise. They are well-tended, and the villagers remit a quarter of the proceeds to Alderley Manor."

"Only one-quarter! I say, your mistress is generous to the point of foolishness."

She shrugged. "It is no more than she needs, and the village is small. Without her largesse, I suspect, Alderley Village would have disappeared years ago. The Manor needs the Village. It is an arrangement that benefits everyone."

"Why not pension the older servants off?"

She shook her head. "That is the way with other households, I am sure, but Alderley Manor is . . . different." A hint of a smile stole onto her face, and a warmth of countenance that irritated him even more than her laugh. "Alderley is . . . home—to everyone here. And one does not leave home simply because one grows old."

"'Forsake not an old friend,'" he began.

". . . for the new is not comparable unto him. A new friend is as new wine. When it is old—"

"—thou shalt drink it with pleasure," he finished.

She looked at him with surprise. "It seems you have not lost all of your memories."

He gave a wry lift of his brow. "Indeed not. I can quote the Bible and speak Latin and Greek, but I confess I would trade those things to know just two words, my true name."

"Do not fret over it. Doubtless it will come to you. Life is too short to spend a second of it worrying."

"Are you always so cheerful?"

She smiled. "Hardly—though I confess it is difficult to remain glum here. Lady Griselda's ceaseless cheer is infectious."

"She sounds full of life."

She laughed. "Oh, indeed! Her ladyship's anthem is 'I will live until I die!'" She thrust her fist defiantly into the air in affectionate parody of her mistress.

He chuckled. "And does her manner of living fulfill that oath?"

"Oh, yes! It always has. She lives each day with a sense of wonder and a feeling that life has good things in store. Everyone here at Alderley does."

"Including you?"

The smile faded from her face. "I suppose so," she

murmured, though he knew instinctively that she was lying. There remained some void in her life, some part of her not content.

He filed the knowledge away.

"So," he prompted, "you *will* call me 'Chris,' then?"

Her smile returned with a wry slant. "You are a persistent man."

"Persistent," he echoed. "I shall add that trait to the list of things I know of myself—a very meager list, at the moment."

"Have patience. Your memory will most likely return in a great rush in a day or two, as Doctor Brown says."

"And it might not."

"Come now, must we add the word 'pessimist' to your list?"

He thought for a moment. "I am afraid we must."

She shook her head. "I was only jesting!"

"Of course, but . . ." He frowned. "Well, truth to tell, I am working on the assumption that I shall never regain my memory, and earlier I assumed the doctor would demand immediate payment."

"That hardly makes you a member of the Pessimists' Guild."

"Oh?" he said, raising one eyebrow. "Only a moment ago, I was begrudging you your pleasant disposition."

"Well," she said, "even that does not make you a pessimist."

"No?"

"No, it makes you a curmudgeon." She smiled.

"Thank you for clearing that up."

"My pleasure." She laughed again.

"My pleasure . . . Chris?" He coaxed.

She sighed and gave a shrug of surrender. "Very well. I shall call you Chris." She gave him a sidelong look. "But only here at Alderley, and only when we are completely alone. Off the grounds or around others, I shall refer to you as 'Mr.' *something*, and if you do not choose a surname, Mr. Something, I will."

"Your name is Julie Williams?"

"Yes."

"Julie—a very nice name. Am I right in hearing it is *Miss* Julie Williams?"

She nodded.

He could sense her sudden shyness, and he was certain that if his sight had been better he would have seen a soft blush creep over her white skin. *Interesting.* Like a bird dog catching a scent, he was suddenly alert.

"Mmm . . . well then, in that case I like your name even better."

She smiled, he thought, and then she looked away, busying herself with rearranging the perfectly arranged breakfast tray. "I—I have a few things to see to," she said. "I will be up to check on you in a little while. Eat slowly, and do not fatigue yourself." She left in a swirl of skirts that smelled of starch and lilac.

No doubt about it.

The chit was aware of him, in a feminine way. He relaxed. No cold haystack and empty belly for him. Not for a while, at least.

Julie shut the door almost to and, taking one last peep through the opening before she left, she well nigh gasped.

"Christopher" was staring at the food with the intensity of a starving man. As she watched, he hunched over the tray and, grasping it reverently with both hands, he closed his eyes and inhaled.

She knew it was an invasion of privacy to watch, but she could not help herself. She was transfixed. She watched as he picked up a thin slice of the buttered toast and placed it tenderly in his mouth. As he bit down, his eyes closed again, and he chewed the bread slowly, worshipfully, as though it were the finest thing he had ever tasted.

She tore her gaze away and glanced guiltily down the hall, grateful it was empty. Reluctantly, she left him. Duty called.

Ordinarily, her daily tasks were enough to keep her busy. Alderley bumped along well enough. The servants, in spite of their age, performed their various duties competently—as long as she was there. But when she was not there—well, that was another matter. The confidence she tried so hard to instill in them seemed to evaporate when she left. Mistakes were made. Tasks were left undone. And if she were away for too long, she returned to chaos.

This time she had been gone nine whole days! She headed for her own bedchamber, shaking her head, knowing with a certainty she'd have nine dozen knots to untangle that day. It would certainly have been easier to face had she a few hours of sleep, but that was out of the question. What was left of the night had been used up in caring for the stranger.

She ducked into her room and quickly undressed, realizing too late there was no water. With a sigh, she dressed again, retrieved water—cold water, since the cook had overslept—and undressed once more. Hastily, she washed and dressed in one of her working gowns, a brown flowered calico. Glancing into the mirror over her dressing table, she frowned, noticing for the first time how plain the gown was. Without thinking, she reached for a necklace of shiny brown topaz.

Her hand stilled.

It was going to be a busy day. She was exhausted, and no doubt she would be working until after sundown. "There is no reason to dress up," she told herself, as an image of the stranger's handsome face floated in her head. "No, no reason at all." She put the necklace down.

A hair-brushing and the addition of a simple, narrow brown ribbon finished the job, and she went downstairs, where all thoughts of the stranger soon flew out of her mind like autumn leaves in the wind.

Chaos reigned, as she expected, and unfortunately it was about to become much worse.

Four

Upon reaching the kitchen, she found Cook attempting to make breakfast with impaired vision, weeping with shame at having overslept. In her haste, the poor old woman had upset the enormous bin of flour, and since she couldn't take the time to clean it up without the meal being even later than it was, her movements about the kitchen were spreading the bumblebroth.

"Oh, Miss Julie," she wailed. "I'm that sorry! What a fearful homecoming for you. Not so much as a hot biscuit to nibble, and then I go and strew this muck all about." Another tear formed in her eye.

"You are not to worry. It is only flour." Julie swiped her finger through the fine dusting of white that covered the tabletop. "We shall soon put it to right."

"You poor mite . . . having to help me when you have so much else to do, what with the visitors and all."

"No hurry. You know Sir Basil keeps Town hours. I daresay we shall not see him before noon, and I have already seen to his—ah . . . his *friend's* breakfast."

"Then you do not know?"

"Know what?"

"Oh, dear," Cook said, looking worried. "I think I had best fetch Lady Griselda." And out she scurried, wiping her floury hands on her apron.

"La," Julie murmured, and braced herself.

Lady Griselda sailed gracefully through the doorway a moment later, followed by a nervous-looking Cook, who flicked her eyes from Julie to Griselda with horrified fascination.

"Oh, my dear, welcome home!" Lady Griselda sang. Her voice was clear and high, like the tone of a silver bell or a bird on a fine spring morning, and she had a figure to match. Tall and fragile-looking, without being frail, she looked dainty and beautiful. Long, thick, flowing white hair entwined with a scarlet ribbon and tiny rosettes that matched her gown adorned her head like a crown. She wore the same expression she always did—a sort of half-smile that always seemed as though she were on the verge of laughter, which she usually was. The fabric of Lady Griselda's life was merriment, the stitchery that held it together, optimism. She was perpetually in a ripping good mood, and her mood was infectious. One could not remain in her company without starting to feel happy oneself—and yet, judging by the look on Cook's face, this time might prove to be the exception.

"I have missed you so." She pressed her cheek against Julie's. "Tell me, were you successful?"

"Yes, I was."

Griselda gave a little gasp of delight. "You found it?"

"Indeed," Julie said. "It was just as you described."

"All red?"

"Even the chimney, though the paint is quite faded."

"Is it still sitting empty?" Griselda asked, her hands working anxiously.

"It is."

"And you made the proper inquiries?"

"Yes. I did just as you instructed, of course."

"Perfect!" Griselda clapped her dainty hands together and smiled. Pure joy radiated from her.

Julie found herself mirroring Griselda's smile. "Perfect for what?" she asked.

"My plan," Griselda said.

"What plan?"

"My greatest adventure."

"Adventure? You have said nothing to me about an adventure."

Just then, an echoing knock sounded through the house.

"Oh!" Griselda cried and clapped her hands together again. "I wonder which one that is?"

"Are you expecting someone?"

"Ah, my dear, indeed I am!" She patted her hair and fussed over her dress. "How do I look?"

"You look very well, but—who is that at the door?"

"No time now. I will tell you all—soon," Griselda promised with a wink and a smile and turned, fairly skipping from the room in her own excitement.

Julie turned to Cook. "Do you know what she is about?"

"No," Cook said, shaking her head. "She's said nought a word about it to me, either, Miss Julie, but whatever it is, it involves a devilish deal of food."

Julie gave her a quizzical look. "Oh?"

"Yes, miss, she said I was to prepare dinner for seventeen—that's including our queer guest upstairs." She tapped her head speakingly.

"Seventeen!"

"Aye. Things will be a touch queer hereabout for a fortnight or so. I've been obliged to double up with Mrs. Bunny and Mrs. Allison, and the menservants have been relocated to the stable house."

"The stable house!" Julie couldn't imagine Griselda having asked any of the servants to move to other rooms. They all lived in comfort in the main house, each in his own private chambers—no drafty garret for the servants of Alderley Manor! And no doubling up or stable houses, either! Was Lady Griselda losing her mind?

"It was our idea," Cook quickly explained, obviously guessing Julie's train of thought. "More rooms were needed for the overnight guests."

"A house party. How long will they be staying?" Whoever *they* were.

"At least a fortnight, the lady says."

"A fortnight!" Julie put her hand to her suddenly aching head. "We do not have provisions for that many for that long. I knew nothing of a house party before I left for Northumberland!"

"None of us did, Miss Julie," Cook said, "but we're all of us making the best of it. It has been a long time since the lady entertained in such a grand way. She is frightfully up in the boughs about it, and, truth to tell, Miss Julie, the rest of us are all sort of excited-like, too."

Julie couldn't help smiling. It was easy to see Cook meant what she said. Her lined face was full of eager anticipation. Whatever this new adventure of Lady Griselda's was, the servants were more than ready to join in the fun. They would follow Griselda over a waterfall, the lot of them laughing all the way.

"The guests are all to arrive today then?"

"All I know is I was told to be ready for seventeen for dinner." Cook clucked softly to herself. "I just wish I knew how many are expected to breakfast!" She turned back to her mixing bowl and continued her work.

Julie left the kitchen and headed for the garden. She needed a moment to think and regroup. Lowering herself tiredly onto the stone bench there, she immediately spied the weeding, deadheading, thinning, and harvesting that needed to be done. *Later.* It would have to be done later, for there was no time now. She took her spectacles off and pinched the bridge of her nose, concentrating on setting priorities.

"La," she told the bees buzzing lazily in the nasturtiums, "I thought nine days' absence was bad, but now nine days might just as well have been nine years." There wasn't enough time to ready the manor for a large house party. "Well then," she said, "I will simply have to work on the most important tasks first." It was the best she could do. "And there will none of it be done just sitting here thinking on it," she said, standing and brushing down her gown.

It was time to set to work.

Chris slept—for how long, he didn't know. The sun was high in the sky when someone knocked softly on the door.

He opened one eye. "Come!"

In came the companion, carrying a large basket in one hand and two pairs of boots in the other. "I am sorry for taking so long to return these to you," she said.

"You have changed clothes. How long have I been asleep?"

"Oh!" she said, guessing his intent, "not long, only a few hours. I put this on"—she smoothed her hand over her skirt—"while you were eating breakfast."

"I do not know why," he said, "for you looked lovely as you were."

She scoffed. "What a ridiculous Banbury tale! You could not even see me clearly, and if you had, you would have seen I looked a fright. I had only just arrived home after more than a week away, and my travelling costume had seen too many miles and too many hours, and then you arrived—"

"For which I apologize."

"La, do not trouble yourself. Trust me," she said, a dimple appearing on her cheek, "you have been the least of my worries this morning." She held out the basket. "This is from the doctor."

Chris took it, peeked in, and pulled forth several pairs of spectacles. Next came a pair of dark brown breeches, a matching coat, two serviceable white shirts that tied at the neck, two white neckcloths, two pairs of stockings, and two brown waistcoats—one dark and one lighter in tone. Small clothes rested at the very bottom of the basket.

"Try them on," she said. "Here, I shall help you."

"Try them on! Here?" he asked, pasting on a deliberately incredulous expression. "Now?"

Her eyes widened, and she held up her palms. "No!" She cried. "No! I was speaking of the spectacles. There are spectacles in that basket . . . several pairs . . . I—I did not mean—"

He threw her what he hoped was a disarming grin and chuckled. "Are you quite sure you would like to help me?"

Instantly, he knew, she realized he had been toying with her. She rolled her eyes. "I will help you with *the spec-ta-cles,*" she said, carefully enunciating each syllable.

"Oh, yes." He molded his face into a mockery of seriousness and winked. "Yes, of course. The spectacles. By all means. You are most kind."

"And you"—she narrowed her eyes at him—"are most incorrigible."

"Guilty as charged, I suppose," he said. "Another personality trait to add to the list. And we should add shameless as well, for my only regret is my faulty eyesight kept me from seeing your expression clearly. I shall have to provoke you thus again when I can see better. Which reminds me"—he extracted the spectacles from the basket—"about those spectacles and the help you offered . . ."

It didn't take them long to discover that the best pair was the pair with the thickest lenses.

"Dr. Brown said to keep the other pairs for a few days. He believes your vision might not have been afflicted before. He believes the lightning may be responsible and that your vision may improve, God willing."

"Whereas I believe," Chris said wryly, "that God has already expressed his will with a bolt of lightning. If that is what damaged my vision, then I do not hold much hope for a miraculous recovery." He shrugged and slipped the appropriate pair of spectacles over his ears and looked upon her clearly at last. Their eyes met, and he allowed his face to break into a smile. It came naturally, for she was charming.

Intelligent, dark green eyes blinked back at him. Her golden brown hair was fine and undisciplined. It had worked itself loose from the knot at the top of her head and caressed the sides of her oval face with shiny curls. Her features were delicate and frank—not quite classically beautiful, but attractive, just the same—and tiny lines crisscrossing an otherwise smooth, creamy complexion suggested she smiled often.

"Whatever I did to anger God must not have carried me beyond redemption, else He would not have brought me to a place of such loveliness," he said staring into her eyes, willing her to know he wasn't referring to the scene outside his window.

He knew instantly she'd taken his meaning, for she blinked and looked away, casting about for something to say. Her eyes found the newspaper, and she gave it a tap. "Doctor Brown thought this might help to shake loose your memories."

"*The Morning Post*," he read.

"Do you recognize it?"

"Is it not"—he took it in hand—"where society turns for society news?"

She nodded. "I suppose—though that is not why Doctor Brown takes it, I am sure. I have never met a man less interested in the intricacies of society. It is most refreshing."

"So you are a social hermit?"

She considered a moment. "I am." She looked down at her hands and changed the subject. "One of the post coaches passes by the head of our lane every day, and the coachman tosses the newspaper down as he drives by. He lives in the next village, Buxley-on-Isis, and he has a large family. The doctor sits vigil whenever his wife gives birth, though thus far she has not needed Doctor Brown's intervention, thank goodness. She just had her thirteenth child two days ago." She tapped the newspaper. "Have a look."

"Monday, August the 10th, 1818," he read and shook his head. "I did not even know the year."

"Then the newspaper has been a help already. How fortunate you remember how to read!" She stood. "Early days, yet. Today's edition is too soon to carry news of your disappearance and a plea for your return, but tomorrow's or the next day's surely will, and Doctor Brown promised to send them up to you as soon as they arrive each day."

He shook his head. "You are assuming I am someone worthy of a search."

"There you are being pessimistic again. There is every reason to believe you are someone of importance. After all, you can read. You are also well spoken, and your inexpressibles are of fine quality."

"Hmm . . . they are also quite shabby, but just before you came in I did discover I know Latin and Greek."

"There! You see? You are an educated man—a merchant, a barrister, a man of the church, a military advisor, perhaps even a peer of the realm. Your family and servants will have missed you by now, and they will turn to the newspapers to find you. You will be reunited with them before long. You are a lucky man."

Again he watched as wistful lines formed upon her brow. It was clearly an expression of sadness, and it wasn't difficult to guess what was in her mind.

"You lost your own family," he murmured.

She gave him a wondering look. "You are perceptive." She moved toward the door, obviously unwilling to speak of it further.

"Wait!" he protested. "Where are you haring off to? Will you not stay and keep me company?"

"I cannot. I have much to do."

"Surely you can spare a half-hour."

"I am sorry."

"What can be so urgent you cannot spend a half-hour buttressing the spirits of an unfortunate wayfarer?"

She laughed. "The wayfarer's luncheon. If I do not go down to the kitchen, you will have none."

"Do you not have a cook?"

"Yes. She is ninety years old, and she naps twice a day." At mention of the word *nap*, her face split into a wide yawn. "Pardon me," she said, "I could use a nap myself. Between my own homecoming, Sir Basil's arrival, and your presence—not that I am complaining, mind you—I am afraid I did not have much sleep last night."

"Did you have any sleep at all?"

She shook her head.

"I thought not."

"La, do I look that bad?"

"Not at all. In fact"—he tapped the wire rim of his spectacles—"the sight of you renders me grateful indeed for these." Immediately, he was rewarded with a rosy blush that spread across her face and down across her chest—though the effect was spoiled with a neckline much too high for his liking. The best one could say of her dress was that it was serviceable, yet she managed to look within an ace of fetching in it.

Fetching, but tired.

"It is just that you look a little sleepy," he said. "Is there no way you can take a short rest?"

She shook her head. "I really must see to luncheon."

"After luncheon, then."

"After luncheon, I must away to the garden. The weeds are staging a revolt."

"Is there no gardener?"

"He cannot stoop. Bad back. From too much weeding, I suppose." She dimpled. "I must also trim the candle wicks, balance the accounts—"

"Let me guess. Rheumatism and bad eyesight?"

She nodded. "That and the fact that we have no butler. Mr. Phelps passed away last year, and Lady

Griselda hasn't wished to cause bad feelings by promoting one footman over another—"

"So the position has gone unfilled?"

Julie nodded. "Yes, but in truth a butler's tasks are not that difficult. Not for me, at least. Oh!" She jumped up. "I forgot to send the menus into the village with Wells! Dear me, where is my head?"

"Why must the menus go to the village, and who is Wells?"

"Wells is a footman, and Lady Griselda has sprung a house party at the last moment. The menus must go to Alderley Village for provisioning. I already sent a preliminary order to the village this morning with the Doctor's housekeeper just to tide us over for the day. I shall have to deliver a revised list later. What cannot be had there we will have to send to London for." She sighed and raked her fingers through her already-mussed honey-colored hair, pulling even more strands free. The effect was charming. "La, there are a thousand things to do." She yawned again.

"You are no mere companion, more like the captain of a ship. Have a care you do not founder onto the rocks, Captain Sleepy."

"Perhaps I shall turn in early this evening," she conceded and then changed the subject, something he was discovering she was adept at. "You slept through luncheon," she said, trying to conceal yet another yawn. "I did not think it wise to awaken you. I will send Mrs. Mapes—she is the housekeeper and a little forgetful, but she does still have good knees and will enjoy being useful—I will send her up with a tray in a few minutes. In the meantime, you must rest."

She made to leave.

"Why are you being kind to me?" he asked suddenly.

She paused and, tilting her head, gave him a quizzical look. "Is there some reason I should not?"

"I am a stranger," he said, "a penniless stranger, with no past and no future. I am a burden, someone to feed, someone to clothe, and when I arrived I looked disreputable indeed—certainly no one with whom people such as yourselves might associate. I can find no reason for the kindness of the doctor, for the kindness of the man who rescued me and delivered me to this place, for the kindness of your unseen mistress who allows me to stay, and most especially not for your kindness."

"A bed and a meal or two would hardly stretch the boundaries of anyone's generosity, Mr. . . . er, Christopher. Pray think nothing of it."

She stopped speaking and, for a moment, gave him a considering, quizzical look. "You are no burden," she said quietly and then quickly quit the room.

He watched her go, confusion nagging at the frayed edges of his limited but growing picture of reality. He was indeed a burden—especially to her. She'd had no sleep last night and today she evidently had no time to spare, and yet she had taken the time to glance in at him as he slept. She had brought the basket and newspaper herself when she could have had them sent up, and—by Jove!—she had even apologized for the amount of time it took to make the delivery.

What does she want from me?

The thought occurred naturally to him, and instantly he wondered why. Why should he question her motives? Was he a man normally surrounded by people with ulterior motives? Was suspicion a normal part of his life?

"I hope to God it is not," he muttered. It did not feel right to suspect Miss Julie Williams. In fact, it felt deuced awful. The only way he could attribute ulterior motives to any of his benefactors was if they knew who he was and were keeping the information from him, but that was not the case. Elsewise, why would they encourage him to read the newspaper? If he were anyone of importance, then certainly there would appear a hue and cry in the newspaper. And if he were someone of no importance . . . well, there would be no reason to conceal his identity then, would there?

No, they *wanted* him to discover his identity, he was certain of it—which led him to another unpleasant thought: What if he failed? What if he never discovered who he really was? What if it turned out he was a nobody and no one came looking for him? It would not be long before he became a burden.

"Well then, Chris old man," he said sitting up, "you had best try to make yourself useful as soon as possible."

Fortunately, it did not sound as though that would be difficult to accomplish there at *Elderly Manner.*

Five

Julie was well nigh in tears.

So far, nine guests had arrived, the lot of them older gentlemen Julie knew to be fond of Griselda. Those who were not calling for hot bathwater, extra pillows, or portable writing desks were behaving like wolves about to quarrel in the drawing room, verbally circling each other and looking for an exposed throat. Luncheon was late, dinner wasn't even on the horizon; it was sprinkling outside and everyone was tracking mud; two horses didn't have a feedbag to call their own; and one of the guests had on so much *eau de cologne* it was making three other guests—and Julie—sneeze. Into the mixture add one Lady Griselda, who flitted from one old man to the other, creating simmering pools of jealous spite in her wake.

"Oh, crumble and bother!" cried Cook at Julie's elbow. They were putting the finishing touches on luncheon. "I think I've gone and burnt the cream sauce."

"Here," Julie said, "let me taste it and—"

Crash!

The unmistakable sound of breaking glass made them jump. Julie burned her hand on the sauce. "What now?" she cried and bolted for the scene of the new chaos, sucking on her smarting finger.

The drawing room floor was covered with glass. Sir Matthew Charles stood at the periphery of the room, a raised walking stick—really a cane—in his hands. Everyone was staring at him, and he looked horrified. "I was demonstrating the proper way to club a golfing ball," he said lamely as Julie rushed into the room.

Some had the good grace to look away and pretend nothing had happened, but others snickered.

Lady Griselda swooped to the rescue. "Cards and tea! We shall have it set up in no time right here. The light in this room is perfect. And we have the most lovely scones. I made them myself, for I confess I have a most out of the common way interest in baking. I hope you do not think that too odd. Who would like a taste?" she asked.

The gentlemen nearly fell over themselves to proclaim their fascination with her culinary pursuits and declare their desire for a taste of any creation of hers. They crowded around her and jostled each other so that Julie worried they would knock each other over—all except for Sir Basil, who obviously would have liked to join in the scrimmage but who had two small dogs in his lap and another much larger creature lying upon his feet. He sat scowling in the corner—though with one hand he was still gently stroking one adoring animal's ears—Lady Cowper, a small white poodle mix who could never have too much attention. Sir Basil's latest addition, she'd been found starving with two dead pups. She was a dear little thing, if one could look past the drool, which was even now water-spotting the settee—not that Julie could worry about that right at that moment, for there were more pressing matters.

There weren't enough scones to go around.

She pinched her nose and wondered how she was going to stop a fight should the old men engage in a round of fisticuffs.

Just then, Lady Griselda's beautiful face emerged from the knot, and her eyes found Julie's. "There *are* enough scones, are there not?" she inquired.

"There are," a strong male voice answered behind her. Julie whirled around. "Christopher!"

"Christopher?" Lady Griselda echoed.

There he stood, dressed in his new clothes, which fit well enough. From the bottom of his black boots to the top of his white neck cloth, he looked every bit the gentleman. He'd obviously washed as best he could, and his still-damp hair and long, handsome sideburns were combed into submission—though Julie suspected they'd go wild once more as soon as they dried. The change was startling. Somehow he managed to look quite respectable.

It was only when one surveyed his face and hand that one found reason for pause—though the spectacles helped, she was sure, for they served to distract the eye from the livid scrape on his cheekbone and the slight swelling of his bruised right jaw. His hand, however, could not be missed, bandaged as it was in white. It was obvious he'd been engaged in a glorious round of fisticuffs. Julie noted more than one pair of raised eyebrows and looks of respect pass across the old gentlemen's faces as they measured his injuries, height, and considerable breadth of shoulder.

All conversation had ceased.

"Er . . . ah . . . Mr. Christopher," Julie said.

"I am Mr. Christopher Christopher, the butler, at your service, gentlemen." He bowed low. "My lady." He strode forward, the ring of older gen-

tlemen dispersing before him like a fog at midday
and, stopping just next to Lady Griselda, he gave
her an elegant deep bow and a surreptitious wink.
The older woman's look of surprise melted, and
she beamed angelically, while the older gentlemen scowled like the devil, and Julie worked hard
to suppress a snicker.

Christopher straightened. "If you will all step into
the library for a few minutes," he said in a resonant
voice while simultaneously herding the dozen in
that direction using nothing outside a commanding
presence, "the drawing room will be set for cards
and tea before long."

Lady Griselda hung back, and when the others
were out of earshot he said to her, "I am honored
to finally make the acquaintance of one to whom I
owe such a debt of gratitude. Your hospitality is most
gracious—and most appreciated."

"Pish-tosh, young man. A few meals and a bed?
Nothing! You are welcome to them. To be perfectly
aboveboard, you are the answer to a prayer. We do
need a butler, as you have evidently discovered, and
as it appears you are willing . . ."

"I am," he said.

"Then in that case welcome home." She patted
him on the cheek, turned on her scarlet leather en-
cased heel, and glided elegantly out of the room.

Sir Basil, still pinned down with Countess
Lieven—seven stone of wolfhound mix—and a lap-
ful of who-knew-what other sorts of mongrels,
watched Lady Griselda, his face stricken. But, without missing a beat, Christopher plucked an apple
from a nearby bowl, gave a whistle, and rolled it
across the floor. Instantly, Sir Basil's lap and feet
were unencumbered as the dogs sprang after the

makeshift ball. Basil smiled with delight and caught up with Lady Griselda in time to offer her his arm as they strolled into the library.

Christopher closed the drawing room door discreetly behind them. "Now for the glass," he said and looked around. "We need more hands."

Mrs. Mapes and Mr. Pinkley both looked to Julie uncertainly.

"Mr. Christopher has volunteered his services as butler," she said. Then she smiled. "He may regret his offer—which we accept unconditionally. Carry on. We have much work to do."

Without another moment's hesitation, Mrs. Mapes bustled off after a broom, and Mr. Pinkley went to summon more help. In no time, Christopher had the servants marshaled and buzzing about the room like an army of happy bees. Card and tea tables were set up, the broken glass, muddy footprints, and drool were cleaned, and two new arrivals were shown to their chambers. Things were running like clockwork. With the addition of *Mr. Christopher Christopher,* twice as much work was done in half the time. And then he did something even more astonishing.

Repairing to the library armed with a tray of brandy snifters, Christopher managed to spill one deftly upon the guest who wore too much cologne.

"Oh, pardon me, sir," the pretend butler said. "If you will follow Wells here, he will show you to your room where a bath will be waiting."

The poor brandy-soaked gentleman had no choice but to comply.

"A bath will be waiting?" Julie hissed. "He is frail, to be sure, but does not move *that* slowly!"

"Perhaps not," Christopher whispered, "but, since

I carried the water up myself a half hour ago, I stand by my word."

"You did what?"

He grinned and winked. "I watered down his cologne, too. He can douse himself with half the bottle and smell no worse than a spray of violets."

She suppressed a chuckle and shook her head appreciatively. "You are amazing," she said, and she meant it. Everything was in order, and the servants had been dispatched on other errands. "You handle people with great skill. I have never produced order and harmony like this"—she gestured about her—"and yet you did so effortlessly."

"I do seem to possess a certain social knack."

"Oh, la! Just one bit of a rub," she said. "The scones."

"What about them?"

"There are not enough to go around."

"There are if you cut them small enough," he said with a smile and a nod toward the plates now resting on the tea tables. There were the scones, cut into pieces small enough so that there were at least three for each guest—and none would dare take more than two.

"You are amazing," she repeated. "You handled Lady Griselda and her guests with the finesse of a title-lofty society host and marshaled the servants with the expertise of a battle-seasoned butler, rather than as one who is still wet behind the ears, and I applaud you—but what on earth are you doing out of bed? The doctor—"

"Said I could rise as soon as I felt up to it." He executed a twirl, and a light hop—on his good foot, she noticed—and clapped his unbandaged hand smartly against the door frame. "I feel fine. The dizziness is gone, the sting is mostly gone from my burns, and Doctor Brown said familiar things might bring back my memory."

"Mmm," she said, noncommittally. If she'd been the doctor, she would not have let him out of bed so soon.

"I have reached a decision," he said.

"Which is?" Julie prompted.

"The chances that I am some duke or bishop or admiral as you have suggested are quite small. I do have a way with people and a rather fine, if worn, pair of breeches, but dukes are not vastly plentiful, whereas butlers and successful merchants are. If I am doomed to live life as a commoner"—he placed one dramatic hand to his brow and then dropped his hand and grinned at her rakishly—"then what better way to bring back my memory than by working as a butler?"

She opened her mouth to protest, but he held up his hand.

"Unless I am some sort of dandy, born and bred to idleness, then I might as well make myself useful with a little work. Where are the scissors?"

"The scissors?"

"You did say the wicks need to be trimmed?"

"Yes, but—but, what if you are a duke? Dukes do not trim wicks."

"Look,"—he rubbed his neck—"if I am a servant, then I will be doing what I am supposed to be doing, and if I am a duke, then we shall all have a famous laugh over this. Put me to work, Captain Sleepy. The scissors, if you please."

"Well . . . as long as you feel up to it, I suppose it cannot hurt, and, truth to tell, I am grateful for any help you can give." She pulled the scissors from her apron and handed them over.

"Good," he said, tucking them into his waistcoat pocket. "Now, about dinner . . ."

Before too long, Christopher had extracted from Julie a list of tasks that needed to be accomplished, assigned himself a portion of them, and had stridden off to complete as many as he could before the evening meal.

Julie, for her part, made for the kitchen where dinner was, thank goodness, on schedule. Into the morning room she went with the book of accounts.

There was much to do to before Alderley Manor would be anywhere near ready for an extended house party. They were not properly equipped, either with servants or foodstuffs. Later she would inquire after some temporary servants down the hill in Alderley Village, and certainly more provisions would soon be needed. The hasty preliminary order she'd sent into the village that morning included only enough to tide the manor over for a day or two.

Fortunately, it was harvest time, and there was a great plenty to go around just then. She dipped her pen and began making a more careful list and then paused and wrinkled her brow. Harvest time meant every able body in the neighborhood would be busy—most likely too busy to help out at Alderley Manor. She sighed and went on with her list. It could not be helped. She would simply have to make do.

Fortunately, she thought with a smile, she was used to doing just that.

The weather was beautiful, one of those mild summer days where a certain crisp breeze in the air presages the autumn to come. The birds were singing in the lindens and chestnuts outside the open window, and she could hear bees buzzing lazily in the hollyhocks across the garden. It felt good to sit down.

Too good. She yawned.

And, in a few moments, Julie had lost her battle with sleep. Her eyes closed, her head sank to the table. She rested her cheek against the cool surface for just . . . a . . . moment—and was gone. Her hands relaxed, and the quill smeared ink over the table.

The buzzing was unmistakable. Someone was snoring. Chris entered the little morning room to investigate and found not some white-haired retainer, but Miss Julie Williams snoozing away. Her golden brown hair, spread across the table, shone like a flow of honey in the afternoon light. The poor thing. She had to be tired indeed to fall asleep in such an uncomfortable place.

He frowned, seeing she'd managed to soak ink into her hair. *Blast.* He'd have to rescue her of course, though he wished he didn't have to. She obviously needed the sleep quite badly, and he hated to wake her.

He needn't have worried.

She didn't awaken when he took the quill from her hand and moved the inkbottle. She didn't awaken when he wiped up the spilled ink from the table or even from her palm and wrist. He shook his head. She was dead to the world.

Extracting his scissors from his waistcoat, he cut away a single lock of ink-soaked hair before the mess could spread. He smiled as he worked. She slept soundly on, blissfully unaware he was staring at her, touching her, thinking about what it would be like to kiss her.

Oh, yes, how could he not think such a thing? Her eyes were closed, her soft pink lips were slightly parted. She smelled warm and sweeter than the fragrance of the honeysuckle wafting through the window. Kissing her was out of the question, of course. Even if she were willing, it would complicate matters.

Wouldn't it?

Oh, yes it would. Whatever else he might be, he wasn't stupid. While the chances were good he'd soon be returning to his own life, the idea that he might not be able to find his way back to wherever he belonged had been plaguing him since he awakened that morning. He had to eat. He had to have a roof over his head. He'd have to find some sort of work somewhere—and Alderley Manor did need a butler.

He'd be stupid to kiss her.

He'd seen the doting way the mistress of the house looked on her companion, the way Miss Williams ruled the roost. One word from her and Lady Griselda would keep Chris as butler—or he'd be out on his arse. He needed to watch himself. No kissing.

"Not yet, anyway," he murmured, "not yet." Not until she wanted him to.

For a moment, his senses went a-begging as his mind followed the thought down a dark hole to its logical conclusion. What if he did kiss her? What if he was the new butler? They'd likely be married.

Is that what he wanted?

What if he never recovered his memory? He could reinvent his life. He could go to the West Indies, to the South Pacific. He could go to America, to India. He could see many things, begin a new life, bed exotic women and eventually marry one.

Or two.

He looked down at Julie. There was nothing exotic about her. She had milky white skin and green-brown eyes. Her features, though pleasing, were nothing to inspire visions of harem dancers or dark-skinned island women. But she was obviously quick-minded and kind . . . and, at the moment, the thought of getting to know her seemed more compelling than the thought of getting to know some exotic temptress.

He snorted. "You have lost your mind as well as your memory, old man."

Julie snuffled in her sleep, and her arm fell off the table. She roughly jerked it back upward and it clopped woodenly back onto the tabletop.

"Ow!" he murmured. Her elbow was going to be bruised. So would her pretty backside and head if she fell from the chair in her sleep.

Making a sudden decision, he moved the adjacent chair aside and deftly scooped the sleeping woman into his arms. As he hoped she would, she snuggled in and slept on.

Limping a little with the extra burden, he carried her to the foot of the stairs, where two servants, two white-haired old ladies, were busy dusting. They rushed toward him, and Chris shushed them urgently.

"Is she hurt?" whispered one, her face full of confusion.

"Poor Miss Julie," the other crooned.

"No, no!" Chris whispered. "She is only asleep!"

"Oh!" they said in unison.

"Where is her chamber?"

"Why, it's . . . it's up the stairs and to the right," one whispered. "Second door on the left."

"Thank you," he mouthed and then began the ascent, cognizant he was leaving the two ladies staring after him, open-mouthed, their ostrich-plume dusters hanging limply at their sides. He supposed it wasn't every day they saw their tireless captain so deeply asleep—but he suspected their open mouths had more to do with the fact that a man was carrying her to her bedchamber. A moment later, the thought was confirmed.

"Mmm-*mmm!*" one said, her soft voice echoing up the stairwell.

"Indeed," said the other.

Chris grinned to himself and kept climbing.

When he reached the top of the stairs, he swayed a little, as a wave of dizziness overcame him, and he clutched at the newel to steady himself. A thrill of alarm bolted through him as he realized he might have tumbled down the stairs with her.

No more carrying lovely damsels for you, old man. At least for a while. He looked down at Miss Williams's smooth, oblivious face. *Too bad,* he thought, *for I find I rather enjoy carrying lovely damsels. This one, at least.*

He lay Julie upon her bed, covered her with a light cotton blanket, and pulled the draperies shut. At the door, he paused and looked about the room. He'd seen her in two gowns, neither of which sported the usual ruffles and lace with which her gender usually adorned themselves. He paused to wonder, suspecting she eschewed ridiculous feminine furbelows for the more practical sort of beauty, and her bedchamber confirmed it. It was appointed with a plain blue counterpane and hangings, simple furnishings, and little else. The only surprise was the large collection of odd vases and gaily colored enamel pots that dotted the room, each filled with sad bouquets, now withered and dried.

He looked over at the sleeping form on the bed. Her face was smooth and peaceful in slumber. He took in her simple gown and even simpler hairstyle. Though a topaz necklace lay on the nightstand, she wore no jewelry whatsoever. She was obviously not one to adorn herself to excess. Her uncluttered dressing table lacked the usual pots and jars he'd have expected to see there—a thought that gave him pause. Just how many ladies' dressing tables had he had the pleasure of perusing?

He raised an eyebrow, filed the thought away, and went back to considering the withered flowers. Julie Williams was a woman of simple tastes. She preferred wildflowers—wildflowers she'd had no time to replenish or even throw out since before she left Alderley . . . how long ago was it? Ten days, he thought she'd said.

Mentally, he added another item to his list of tasks to complete and quit the room, closing the door silently behind him.

Six

Note sent from Bedford to London:

We picked up her trail in Bedford where she turned south and east. We will follow. You will no doubt find it queer to hear we had it from the ostler here her footmen said she had been up near Gretna seeking a house to let. Mayhap you will want to send someone to follow her trail back north quick as may be and pay extra for the advice we trust.

Julie awakened with a start. "Where am I?"

Her room!

She sat bolt upright. "How in the world did I get here—and how long have I slept?" She flew to the window and, pulling back the draperies, was assailed by the unmistakable gleam of morning light. She'd slept all night? "Oh, la!" she cried.

Off came the rumpled brown calico. Julie dressed as quickly as she could in a simple blue gown with short puffed sleeves. Her hair was a mull and required more time than usual, time she begrudged. What was happening downstairs? How had dinner come off the night before? The house seemed awfully quiet. She pulled on fresh stockings and rolled her eyes. "Perhaps they have all killed each other!"

She wondered if all the guests had arrived. It was

beyond her what had possessed Lady Griselda to invite that particular group—Mrs. Ophelia Robertson, her husband John, and twelve other old gentlemen.

"Twelve *love-struck* old gentlemen," Julie corrected herself aloud. Surely, it was a recipe for a highly unsettling house party, if not for outright disaster, in spite of the grace inherent in the hostess.

Lady Griselda was a man magnet and apparently always had been, though she'd never married. Slender and beautiful, she laughed often and floated freely from one subject to the next, rarely completing a thought—though the men she collected like stray buttons didn't seem to notice.

Julie pinned her hair back and finished it off with a wide blue ribbon, took a pair of crocheted gloves and a straw bonnet from the wardrobe, and stuck her feet into her walking shoes, knowing she'd have to journey to Alderley Village later to carry the order and see about more servants. Only then did she notice that her room was filled with flowers.

Her old dead bouquets had been replaced with all new bunches of scotch bluebells and daisies, eyebrights and forget-me-nots. She smiled, wondering which of the servants was responsible for the deed.

She sighed with pleasure and quit the chamber.

A quick survey of the downstairs rooms showed the house in order and nearly empty but for the drawing room, where the guests played at cards.

Julie retrieved her unfinished food list and made for the kitchen. It was tidy, the morning meal was over, and Cook was taking her mid-morning nap. Julie quickly finished the list as she broke her fast and then packed up a basket of food to take to the coachman's wife. Mrs. Bloom had given birth only three days before and needed looking in upon. Tucking the list into her reticule, she rose.

Passing the library doors on the way outside, she caught sight of one white-haired old man looking out of the tall library window.

"Good morning, Sir Basil," Julie greeted the familiar silhouette.

"Ah, good morning Miss Williams," he said amiably enough, but his eyes never left the lawn outside.

"What are you watching?" she asked, coming to stand beside him.

"Him." Sir Basil tapped the windowsill. "My new kennel master."

Julie looked outside. There, to her surprise, stood Christopher with Sir Basil's ladies. He was next to a stone bench, tossing sticks for the dogs to retrieve. One dog, Lady Sefton, wasn't playing. True to her namesake, she was a sweet natured thing, and never vastly energetic. She lay on the bench, her head hanging over the edge. As they watched, Christopher reached over and absently patted the dog's head. When Princess Esterhazy and Countess Lieven began quarreling over a stick, a sharp command settled the matter immediately. The rest of the dogs frisked happily about, grinning with their tongues hanging out.

"It looks as though Mr. Christopher is enjoying the outing as much as any of your ladies."

"Yes, he is quite good with them," Sir Basil said, "which is why I hired him."

"Hired him?"

"Yes. Need someone to watch the ladies while I pay attention to . . . other things."

Julie looked at him sharply. What other things could possibly distract Sir Basil's attention away from his beloved companions?

"Sir Basil," Griselda called, sailing into the room behind them, "our opponents are becoming restless, and—ah, there you are, Julie. I was beginning to wonder if you would rise at all this day. I wondered if you might sleep right through to the morrow. I thought I might have to send the servants to your chamber, each carrying a bell." She pointed to the mantel, where rested a large collection of silver bells, all given to her over the years by Sir Basil, who acquired at least one wherever he traveled.

Julie felt herself blush. "Do forgive the late hour, Lady Griselda, I—"

"Pish-tosh, dear. Of course you were exhausted from your trip and from staying up with the invalid. Speaking of whom,"—she peered out the window—"he seems to be right enough now."

"All but his memory," Sir Basil said. "It has not returned."

"The poor boy," Griselda cooed.

Julie gestured toward him. "Has Doctor Brown sent up a newspaper this morning?"

"He has," Sir Basil said with a look at Griselda, "but I am afraid I spilled creamed herring all over it and the ladies devoured it."

"The ladies ate the newspaper?" Julie asked, incredulous.

"Some. The rest they tore to shreds," Sir Basil said, "But I had already read it. Mr. Christopher would have found nothing to satisfy him there. I told him so just a short while ago."

"You should have seen him," Griselda said, shaking her head sadly. "Dreadfully disappointed. Poor boy," she said again. "If he were titled or devilish wealthy, surely some word of his disappearance would have appeared in the papers by now."

"Mmm." Sir Basil nodded. "Quite a blow to a man's pride, I should think. One day anything seems possible, being a gentleman or a famous explorer or anything else the imagination can conjure—"

"And the next he finds he is of no importance to anyone," Griselda finished. "Poor, poor boy."

"Who?" Ophelia Robertson demanded, her spray of magenta ostrich feathers waving atop her head as she came into the room behind them.

"Mr. Christopher, Ophelia," said Lady Griselda. "The one I told you about."

Mrs. Robertson's mouth formed a small *o*, and she followed her friend's gaze outside toward the bench. "That him?" she asked.

Griselda nodded.

"Who?" Mr. John Robertson said, entering the library. He wore riding boots, and his gray hair was windblown.

Ophelia traded a speaking look with Griselda and swayed off to greet her husband. "No one, my beloved. My, but you do look handsome when you have been out riding."

"Heh," he remarked skeptically, but he smiled down at her fondly and pinched her cheek just the same. It was easy to see they were very much in love.

"Well," Sir Basil said, turning to Griselda, "I daresay we have done all we can for him for now, and now that I have checked on my ladies, I can return to our game. Pray accept my apology for the interruption."

"Pish-tosh," his hostess said, "it could not be helped."

Sir Basil smiled gratefully. "Would you care to join us, my dear?" he asked Julie.

"No, thank you," she said. There was too much to be done. "Another time, perhaps."

Sir Basil offered Lady Griselda his arm, which she accepted with a sweet smile, and they moved off with the Robertsons toward the card room. Julie pulled on her gloves, tied on her bonnet, and slipped outside.

The weather was fine again that day. A cool breeze sifted through the leaves overhead as she walked toward Christopher's bench. The ladies greeted her happily as they always did, and Christopher smiled.

"They like you," he called.

She laughed. "It is because I always give them something to eat. I am afraid I must disappoint them this morning, however. I was too rushed to think of it."

"Where are you haring off to in such a hurry?" he asked.

"To Doctor Brown's and then to the village."

"Would you mind if I came along?" He looked down at the dogs and smiled. "If *we* came along," he corrected.

"By all means. I should welcome the company"— she chuckled—"the lot of it. Shall we?" She gestured toward the lane, and Christopher fell into step beside her.

"You look well enough," Doctor Brown said at his door, eyeing Chris critically. "Burns healing?"

"A little sore," Chris answered, "nothing more."

"Mmmm . . ." the physician intoned.

Actually, the burns, particularly the one on his hand, hurt like hell, but there was no way he was going to say so, especially in front of Julie.

Doctor Brown seemed to understand that. "Just watch for signs of infection. Any heat, any redness, and I want you down here"—his eyes flicked toward Julie—"no matter what. Understand?"

Chris nodded, and Doctor Brown turned to Julie. "Going into the Village today?"

"Yes."

"I am off to Buxley-on-Isis to see to some patients there. Would you look in on Mrs. Bloom as you pass?"

She smiled. "I was already planning on it."

A hint of an answering smile crossed his features. "Some people do not know their place."

"And some people," she responded, "do not fool anyone. Goodbye!"

Chris fell into step beside her. "What was that about?" he asked.

Julie told him of her interest in medicine. "But I cannot be a physician, of course," she said, kicking at a stone. "Doctor Brown knows I would find his sympathy on that score intolerable, and yet ignoring it would be awkward, so he needles me about it to be kind."

"With friends like that . . ." Chris began.

She laughed. "Do not misunderstand. Doctor Brown is a good man—and a dear friend."

Chris couldn't resist. "Could he ever be more?"

"No!" she said. "Never."

The force of her response surprised him. Why such vehemence? Clearly, she admired the doctor, who by his own admission was not averse to pursuing her. The number of potential husbands was limited in small villages. Could it be she had found someone else she fancied even more than the doctor, or was it that she hated the idea of marriage altogether? He filed the question away. Now was not the time to ask.

They walked on in companionable silence for a time. Though the sun was long up and the wind was rising, fog still clung between the hedgerows and in the hollows. Birds sung merrily in the tree-tops. It was Chris's favorite time of day, though he had the feeling it had been a long time since he had been up that early. He wondered why. Was he used to keeping Town hours?

It felt good to be taking a walk. Especially with company. It felt . . . right somehow, perfect. And completely foreign.

"The newspaper was of no help this morning," he said.

"Have you remembered nothing more on your own?"

He shook his head. "Not really. A few random images. In the stables this morning, I remembered a carriage. It was a smart thing with yellow seats and silver trimming—though I do not know whose it was. And last night, as I lay in bed, I remembered—" He could not tell her what he remembered, for it was nothing a lady should hear. "I remembered lying in a large bed with pink lace hangings," he finished, which was true enough.

"Pink lace!" She gave him an odd look.

He shrugged. "I have no idea where it was, or even if it is a true memory and not something my mind conjured." Also true. "It is difficult to separate snippets of memory from mere thought, impossible to know which is which."

"It must be vastly frustrating," she said, her voice kind.

He nodded.

A few seconds passed. The dogs ducked in and out between the hedgerows, wagging their tails and sniffing the air. One gave a yelp and shot off across the meadow, chasing an imaginary something, and the rest followed, baying madly.

Chris chuckled. "I do not know who is enjoying the walk more, Sir Basil's ladies or their caretaker."

"Sir Basil told me he offered you the position of kennel master."

"It is temporary, only until I find another situation. He does not really need me. I am right and tight the offer was made only to spare my dignity."

"Sir Basil is a good man," she said quietly, "though I daresay he is lucky enough to employ you, even temporarily. I should think a man with your education and manner could find any number of positions elsewhere. Excellent positions."

"Such as butler in a country house?" he asked.

She dimpled. "Am I that transparent?"

"You are." He laughed. "And I take no offence. You are kind to think of my welfare, and I thank you, but . . ." He coughed. "After Lady Griselda's lightning-quick assessment and welcome yesterday, you might suppose the position is mine should I wish it. But I think Lady Griselda no longer shares your good opinion of me."

"Why ever not?"

"Well," he said, "yesterday, after I carried you up to bed—"

"*You* carried me?" Her marvelous green eyes widened, and her ears turned pink.

"Did you think perhaps Wells had done so? Or Mr. Sully?"

In spite of her obvious embarrassment, she chuckled. "No. I had assumed—or hoped, rather!—that I walked in my sleep."

"Sorry to disappoint," he said.

"You must be able to move like a wraith. I am not a sound sleeper."

"Oho! You were yesterday. Sound enough for me to return three times delivering flowers."

"You?" she cried. "Thank you!"

"You had been kind to me," he said with a shrug, "and I had nothing with which to repay you. The flowers were but a trifle, and unfortunately they turned out to be the only thing of worth I did for you yesterday."

"What do you mean?" she asked.

"Do you recall I was going to help you? To serve as *de facto* butler?"

She nodded. "Of course I accepted and then promptly fell asleep. How embarrassing!"

"Not," he said, "as embarrassing as what I did."

Her eyes grew wide. "What did you do?"

"I attempted to complete your figures in the ledger."

She looked confused. "And?"

"And I do not know a ledger from a teapot, it seems. I am afraid I made a muck of it."

"La, that is nothing. I am sure I can straighten it out."

"Ah, but ledgers are not the only thing at which I am inept. It seems I can recognize ripping good horseflesh but cannot groom one properly—or so your Mr. Sully tells me. He also said I lift heavy objects with my back, not my legs. I trim candlewicks so short they cannot be lit, and the fires I build smoke so that the rooms must be cleared. Supper last night was served quite late, I am afraid."

He braced himself for rebuke or at the very least sharp criticism of his mistakes, but to his surprise Miss Williams did neither of those things.

"I suppose it is difficult to see one's meal when the room is pitch black and smoky." She laughed. "How did the guests react?"

"I think none of them realized anything was amiss. I ushered them outside for a stroll until the house could be aired—thank heavens for the moon, which was waxing toward full!—and when I came to retrieve them, Lady Griselda had the lot of the gentlemen participating in a nighttime scavenger hunt like excited children."

"I am not surprised," Julie said. "Gentlemen adore Lady Griselda and follow her as eagerly as the ladies follow Sir Basil. They would walk through fire gleefully if she asked them to and swear they had fun doing so."

Her face registered merriment, but then it slowly crumpled into concern.

"Something bothering you?" he asked.

"No . . . not really. I just wonder what possessed Lady Griselda to construct the guest list as she did. Do you know, five more gentlemen are expected today?"

"Two of them arrived yesterday on the heels of a lady. Mrs. Robertson, I believe her name was."

She nodded. "Ophelia Robertson—Lady Griselda's chaperone, I believe—though Mrs. Robertson is not the one I would have chosen for her."

"Why not?"

"Well . . . Mrs. Robertson is a dear, to be sure. I have known her for some time now, and I admire her for many reasons. But Mrs. Robertson is . . . well, Mrs. Robertson. She defies description. Polite description." She gave a wry smile. "The truth is—and I am not telling you anything that is not common knowledge—

Mrs. Robertson is considered a little . . . *fast.* She is a wealthy old spinster—or was until she married a family servant five years ago."

"Not *John* Robertson?" he cried.

"You have met him then?"

He laughed. "I did indeed, but I thought he was a servant who just happened to share Mrs. Robertson's surname." He shook his head. "He alighted from the coach and headed for the stables to take care of the horses, he said. The servants were all quite happy to see him. Apparently he is quite popular."

"He is a good man," she said with a strongly affirmative nod, "as measured and unobtrusive as his wife is outrageous, flamboyant. She is certainly not a steadying influence. I am worried. Inviting twelve gentlemen and only one lady is queer as dick's hatband, even for Lady Griselda."

"The lady often engages in unconventional behavior, then?"

"Oh, la, I *have* spoken out of turn. You are unaware of Lady Griselda's habits."

"Oh la," he echoed comically, "if she is often that way, then her staff knows all there is to know, and since I am *or was*"—he threw her a deliberately mischievous grin—"her butler. . . . Well, I hardly think you can have spoken out of turn, since a good butler knows *everything* there is to know about the household he so benevolently rules." He sobered then and gave her a reassuring nod. "Really, I hardly think you have spoken out of turn, and I do not question your loyalty to her."

"And indeed you should not," she said. "My feelings for my employer go beyond loyalty. I love her dearly."

He nodded.

"There," she said, waving a slender white gloved hand off to the right. "The Blooms' place. I must stop there for a few minutes. I hope you do not mind."

Chris shook his head, and Julie led the way down a well-worn footpath into a foggy, tree-lined dell where stood a small thatched cottage and a half dozen other crude buildings—barns and storage sheds, Chris assumed, though they did not look much different from the cottage.

"You should probably wait outside," Julie said quietly as they approached. "Mrs. Bloom gave birth to her thirteenth child three days ago. She might still be abed, and as it is a small house. . . ."

"I understand," he said and veered off to stand at the side of the bare, hard-packed dooryard as she went up to knock.

An older child, a girl of perhaps eleven years, answered the door. Her face lit up. "Good morning, miss. Mama, it's Miss Julie!"

"Come in, come in!" a feminine voice rang out, and Julie stepped inside, but before the door closed the girl caught sight of Chris, and it was not long before the door opened once more.

Out spilled seven bantlings of various ages, who clustered around Chris to satisfy the curiosity rampant in their expressions. Who was he? Was he a friend of Miss Julie's? Was he going to stay a while? And the most important question, it seemed: Would he like to play?

So far, his surroundings and circumstances had not seemed completely unfamiliar—mealtimes, the workings of the household, everyday tasks. While he was sure he'd not been in Alderley before, he was sure he'd been somewhere like it before, and while he didn't remember what sort of clothing he'd been used to wearing, he still remembered how to button his breeches.

But children!

He was a fish out of water.

Though all Mrs. Bloom's labors were blessedly easy, she'd had a few difficult recoveries, and Julie was relieved to see this was not one of them. She had stayed abed, as Doctor Brown had ordered her to, and there were no signs of fever. The babe, a large fine boy, appeared well, too. Julie unpacked the basket she'd brought, and served some soup from the kettle over the fire to Mrs. Bloom along with some of the cheese and apples she'd brought.

Taking the baby in hand so a grateful Mrs. Bloom could eat undisturbed, she wandered to the door and out into the yard, where she'd heard the children playing.

She froze and stared in wonder.

Christopher was playing, too.

He was blindfolded and most of the younger children were dashing this way and that, taunting him gleefully and shrieking with laughing delight as he tried to catch them. And they weren't the only ones laughing. Christopher was laughing so hard Julie didn't know how he kept to his feet. And then, he didn't! Dropping to his knees in the middle of the yard, he clutched at his belly and kept right on laughing. The children all piled on top of him, and in a few seconds they were a squirming knot of arms and legs and giggling, smiling faces.

Julie put her hand to her mouth and laughed right along.

Somehow, Christopher extricated himself from the pile first, taking his blindfold off and emerging with a grin still on his face. Sir Basil's ladies chose that moment to race into the scene, and the children, shrieking with delight, untangled themselves and ran off pell-mell with Christopher's handkerchief, which had fallen from his pocket. The dogs raced after the children, barking excitedly, and Christopher smiled after them and strode over to Julie, brushing dust from his clothes.

"Beyond repair, I think," he said, looking down at his waistcoat and breeches. "They will have to be washed."

"You do not look a bit contrite," she said, laughing.

His eyes danced. "Not a bit," he agreed.

"I think you have seven new friends."

"I hope so," he said. Then he turned attention to Julie's cargo, bowed and took the baby's tiny hand. "Pardon me, madam," he addressed the infant. "We have not been properly introduced."

"Sir," Julie corrected in comic aside. "Pardon me, *sir.*"

"Oh, you really must pardon me then, *sir.*" He gave another bow.

Julie laughed. "Mr. Christopher Christopher, may I present Mr. Augustus Bloom, the latest—"

Crash!

The sound came from inside the cottage. "Oh, la!" Julie cried, "Mrs. Bloom!" She thrust the baby into Christopher's arms.

He looked down at the child and grimaced. "But—but I do not know how to—"

"Just hold him!"

The baby started, filled his lungs, and wailed as only a tiny baby can. Christopher looked stricken. "What do I do?"

"Sing him a lullaby!" she called over her shoulder and ran into the house.

Seven

Thank God it was only spilled soup. Mrs. Bloom had dropped her bowl and then, getting up to clean it, she'd knocked over a table.

Julie saw Mrs. Bloom back to bed, cleaned up the soup and righted the table, and then went outside to retrieve the baby.

For the second time that day, she froze.

There was Christopher holding the baby. He hadn't noticed the door open, hadn't noticed her step outside. She didn't think he'd notice if an elephant paraded by.

He stared down at the baby in his arms with a reverent smile—in spite of the baby's hold on Christopher's nose.

Christopher was bouncing rhythmically the way all adults inevitably do with babies in their arms, and he was singing, just as she'd suggested he do, in a sweet, soothing rhythm. It was a few seconds before she recognized the tune.

It wasn't exactly a lullaby.

> *"A sup of good whiskey will make you glad*
> *Too much of the creature will set you mad.*
> *Yet father and mother,*
> *And sister and brother,*

> *They all take a sup in their turn, hey-o!*
> *They all take a sup in their turn!"*

"What sort of lullaby is that?" Julie asked, coming along beside him.

"The only sort I know, it seems," he said sheepishly. "Look, there is something all out with this child. The poor thing has the pox or something, and it is all floppy."

"Pox! You cannot be serious. I looked him over myself, and he has no—"

"Here." Christopher pulled back the blanket and pointed at the tiny white bumps on the baby's face. "And its skin is coming off its head. Pox and leprosy, maybe."

"Give him to me," Julie said, holding her arms out and chuckling.

But Christopher pulled away from her, an expression of alarm on his face. "No! You should not be holding him. It might be catching."

"You are serious! La, I thought you were joking. Christopher, babies often have these white bumps on their faces. And the *leprosy*, as you call it, is nothing but cradle cap. It will go away before long." She took the baby from him. "He is only a few days old. His umbilical cord hasn't even come loose yet."

"He still has one of those things attached?" he asked with a shudder.

She snorted. "You really are new at this. All infants have them. They go away—just like the cradle cap and the little white bumps."

Julie took the baby back to his mother and emerged. Chris smiled and fell into step beside her. The rising sun was just peeking over the rim of the Blooms' little dell. It kissed his dark blonde curls, firing them with gold. "Ready?" she asked.

"The children still have my handkerchief," he said, looking around. "I think the idea was to keep it from me, but they did not bring it back."

"Hide and seek. It is a game children play. You have forgotten it, evidently."

He said nothing, and they walked along in silence for a minute or two. Julie could almost feel Christopher pondering. His bearing and expression had turned pensive.

"The baby truly is well, if that is what is bothering you," she said.

"Am I that transparent?"

"As a summer sky," she told him.

"I am not worried about the baby. I trust your judgement."

"Then, pray, what troubles you?"

"The children," he answered, "and the games."

"What about them?"

"Well . . . do all children learn to play this *blind man's buff*?"

"I—I suppose so," she answered. "I did, and I was an only child and very isolated. I had no playmates, ever—but I learned to play games from the servants."

"And *hide-and-seek*?"

She nodded. "That one too. I cannot imagine any child not learning that."

"I did not."

She stared at him. "How can you know that? You have lost your memories. Christopher! Have you remembered something? Have you remembered *everything*?" She felt a sweet gladness soar up inside her—and then realized with a rush that if his memory had returned he'd be leaving, likely today.

"No," he said, oblivious to her wildly beating heart. "No, I have remembered nothing more. But the children had to teach me to play blind man's buff—and I still do not know how to play your hide-and-seek."

"But you have lost your memory."

He looked at her gravely. "You do not understand. I know the complete rules of whist, hazard, faro, and piquet."

Understanding washed over her. "La! It is reasonable to conclude you have never been exposed to other children."

He nodded.

"Ohh . . . and then there was your lullaby and your ignorance of babies."

"Indeed. From which we may conclude I must be green with children *and* babies."

"So you probably have no siblings much younger than you."

"And no children of my own, most like."

Julie allowed that it must be true. How else could they explain his lack of knowledge?

They mulled it over silently, each to themselves as they walked the rest of the way into Alderley Village.

"Babies are always floppy," she said at last.

"Are they always that sweet-smelling?"

She laughed. "Hardly."

"How do I get my handkerchief back?"

"You will have to go back to the Blooms' place, I suppose."

He smiled. "I shall look forward to it," he said, and Julie was certain he meant it.

The village hummed with activity, as everyone rushed to fill the orders from Alderley Manor. Chris accompanied Miss Williams as she added last-minute items to the orders and arranged for delivery. She also attempted to engage more servants while she was there, but with harvest beginning, no one was available.

"I admire your restraint," he said as they walked out of the village and down the lane toward Alderley Manor.

She gave him a quizzical look.

"I expected you to bluster and make demands back there."

"Why would I do such a thing?"

"Why?" He shook his head. "You cannot be serious. Julie, Alderley Manor holds the cards. Lady Griselda owns the village flock, the village fields, the village orchards. The villagers should be bending over backward to help in any way they can—even if they find it odious for whatever reason. What are you planning to do about it?"

"Do?" she asked. "What *can* I do about it? The wheat is ripe. Harvest cannot be delayed simply because Lady Griselda chooses to have an inconvenient house party."

"You could insist upon help. The villagers could put in extra hours at harvest in order to help up at Alderley. I expected you to demand it."

She tilted her head. "You seem to expect me to behave badly."

He thought for a moment. "You are right. By Jove, you are right. I do expect you to behave badly, and—and I do not know why. Forgive me. You have shown me nothing but kindness. There is no reason to expect you to behave in any other way."

"Forgive *me*, Christopher, but you seem surprised and disproportionately grateful for the smallest of kindnesses. I begin to think you are not used to such treatment—from anyone."

The same thought had occurred to Chris—but now another, more disturbing thought assailed him. Perhaps he *wasn't* used to being treated badly. Perhaps *he* was used to treating others that way.

He said nothing about it. What was there to say?

They passed the mill, a small inn, a row of tidy cottages, and then the church. "Is that where the wedding will be?" Chris asked.

Miss Williams stopped right in the middle of the lane. "What wedding?"

"Why . . . Lady Griselda's, of course."

She froze. Her eyes grew round, and her mouth gaped. "Lady Griselda? She is to be married?"

"You did not know?"

"No," she murmured, shaking her head. "No, she never mentioned it to me. Wh-whom is she marrying?"

Chris shrugged. "I do not know—one of the guests, I believe—but I do know the wedding is to take place at the end of the house party."

She blenched. Without another word, she turned and struck out for home.

It was no great distance from the village to Alderley Manor—which was a good thing, because Chris had to run to keep up with her.

Eight

Julie swept into the house and through the front hall, garnering odd looks from a servant and two guests. She didn't care.

"Where is Lady Griselda?" she asked.

"What?" Mrs. Wentworth, the downstairs maid, asked. She was quite deaf.

"Lady Griselda," Julie said, carefully and loudly enunciating the words.

"I am here, my dear—in my private salon!" Griselda's voice rang out loud and clear. "Why ever are you shouting?" She emerged from the salon and came toward Julie with a smile on her face, her lovely alabaster skin glowing with its usual faint natural blush.

Julie blinked and made for her, looped her arm through Griselda's, and drew her into the nearest empty room, the library. She closed the door calmly enough, though she felt more like an angry child inside, a child who wanted to run about and shout and ring the bells on the mantel angrily. How could Griselda not tell Julie she was planning to wed? Did she not know she was as much mother as she was friend to Julie? Julie willed herself to be reasonable and adult, but Griselda's face conveyed worry anyway.

"What is the matter, dearest?"

"Is it true? Are you to be married?"

She looked confused. "I did not tell you? Oh, dear me! That is beyond hen-witted. Even for me." Her smile appeared once more, like a sunrise after a storm. "Oh, but Julie, is it not wonderful?" She clasped her hands and twirled around. "I am to be married!" she said rapturously.

Julie sat heavily on a nearby sofa. "To one of the guests?"

"Of course. They are my favorite dozen. I have invited them here in order to decide which of them will make me the happiest of women."

The room began to spin. Julie had assumed that one of the guests had already proposed. "There has been no proposal?"

"No . . . well . . . yes. Dozens, actually. Every one of my dozen has asked at one time or another, but I have not accepted any of them yet, of course."

Julie clutched at the arm of the chair, feeling as though she might fall. "You have them here to choose which of them to wed?"

Griselda nodded and smiled. "Of course. Did I not already say that? Did you not wonder why I invited them all here?"

Julie ignored the question. "Do they all know why they are here?"

She nodded. "Indeed—though they do not know the method I am using to make my choice."

"Method?"

"Wedding charms," she said as though she'd said nothing remarkable. "Ophelia brought them to me. And they will reveal to me the man I am destined to marry," she went on breezily. "Ophelia acquired the medallions from Artemis Chase, the Countess of Lindenshire."

"'The Gypsy'?"

"None other."

The countess, a Gypsy maid who had married the *ton's* most eligible *parti* early in the past year, had made quite a splash among the *ton*. Julie had heard tales of the woman from Sir. The Gypsy was wont to read palms and tea leaves wherever she went.

Julie pushed her spectacles up and tried not to press her brows together. "What will you do with these medallions of Lady Lindenshire's?" she asked.

"They are rather small, you see,"—Griselda held out two fingers—"and they are made of gold. And it is bad luck for my husband-to-be to see them before he takes a bite," she said as though that explained everything.

The entire world was spinning now. "A bite?" Julie asked weakly.

"A bite of my lemon tart. It is my best dessert."

"You plan to put one of the charms in the lemon tart?"

"Both of them actually, but of course I will make sure I am served one of the medallions myself. The other I shall leave up to fate to place. Fate will choose wisely for me."

Julie shook her head. "No . . ."

"Why, whatever is wrong, my dear?" Griselda said, her face folding into uncharacteristic lines of concern.

"What is wrong?" Julie cried. "What is wrong? Everything! Everything is wrong! You cannot marry!"

"Why not?"

"Why should you? Griselda, you are wealthy, independent. You do not need a man to take care of you."

Griselda put her hand to her mouth. "A man to take care of me, no—but a man to love me . . ."

"But you already have people who love you. The—the servants," she stammered, "the villagers, and . . . and me." To her consternation, she felt tears pricking her eyes.

"Darling," Griselda said, not unkindly, "it is not that I do not value your love, but you must admit that the love of friends—even dear ones such as yourself—is vastly different from the love of a man."

"But each one of the dozen love you. They have for years. How many times have they proposed to you?"

"Oh," Griselda said with a girlish giggle, "a few."

"A few score, more like."

Griselda dimpled. "Perhaps."

Julie went forward and clasped the older woman's birdlike hands. "Do you not see, dearest lady? You already enjoy the love of a man. Many men. Would you give that up?"

Griselda sighed and her smile faded like a rainbow from the sky. "I know you value independence, Julie," she said gently, "and I admire you greatly for it. Leaving your uncle's house and striking out on your own under an assumed name—it was nothing short of courageous."

Julie wondered what praise—or pity—Griselda would heap on her if she knew Julie had married a blackguard to save her fortune. She hadn't told Griselda about the marriage. Mrs. Robertson had arranged everything, but Julie had sworn her to silence. She hadn't wished to worry Griselda before the fact, and afterwards the wedding was something she'd desperately wanted to forget.

Griselda patted her hand. "I believe I have never

known another woman whose resolve was stronger. You did not, as many young ladies would have done in your place, wait around to be saved. You saved yourself, and I am enormously proud to call you friend."

Julie shook her head. "No. No, you have it all wide of the mark. It was you saved me. You offered me a position without more than a glance, on Mrs. Robertson's recommendation."

"Then I suppose we saved each other, darling, though it seems to me I am the better off for the bargain, for all I gave you was a place to live, while you gave me the greatest friend I have ever had."

Julie's eyes misted, and she closed them to keep herself from crying.

"Oh . . . I see," Griselda said suddenly. "Or do I? Do you fear I will ask you to leave after I marry? I could never do that!"

Julie's eyes snapped open. "No. But your husband may."

"He could," Griselda conceded grimly. "He could indeed. Mind you, I do not think for a moment that any of the dozen would do such a thing, but I must admit that he could if he wanted to. Husbands can do whatever they wish."

"Then why marry?" Julie cried.

Griselda sighed again. "You still do not understand." She sat heavily on the sofa, seeming tired suddenly, tired and grim.

Julie sat next to her.

Griselda smiled sadly. "I am older," she said. "You are an intelligent young woman. It must have occurred to you how few years I have left."

Julie began to protest, but Griselda held up one palm to silence her.

"Let us not offer each other false denials," she said. "We do not need them. We have always shared the truth, you and I." She searched Julie's eyes, her gaze piercing and intense. At last, Julie gave a quick nod, and Griselda squeezed her hand. "Smart gel." She settled back into the sofa. "I have had a wonderful life, full and rich. Free from want and worry. I have traveled whenever and wherever my fancy has led. I have explored jungles and caves and beaches and wild moors . . . ah, Julie, the things I have seen!

"And, yes, I now enjoy the love and company of many fine people—but I must tell you it has always been so. I love people. Women . . . children . . . men—especially men." She bit her lip and dropped her gaze before going on. "It may shock you to hear this, but you must understand . . ." Her voice trailed off.

She appeared to consider for a moment and then looked Julie solidly in the eyes as she said, "I am not marrying merely to taste the carnal pleasures. I have tasted them." She gave an unladylike snort. "I have devoured them, more like."

Her eyes took on a faraway look, and Julie could only stare in fascination. Griselda gave a dreamy laugh. "Oh, Julie . . . from that first handsome stable boy when I was a girl right up until I tutored a certain young duke last year, my life has been one glorious feast!"

Julie blinked in shock at the frankness of the admission.

Griselda went on. "I have lived my life as I have wished, my dear, always. I have done things my way, always, whatever I wished and whenever I wished.

"The one thing I have not done is share my

heart." Her old face took on an almost unbearable sadness.

"Husbands have the power to dominate their wives completely. To direct their lives in the most minute fashion. To control them. Even to imprison them, beat them. I know you will protest it is too risky to place such power in the hands of any man, that no man can be trusted, and five years ago I would have agreed with you."

"What has happened to change your mind?" Julie asked.

"Ophelia and John Robertson happened. They are so very happy."

Julie had to concede that they did, indeed, appear to be well-suited for each other.

"But it is more than that," Griselda said. "Can you not see they love each other? Do you not see the fun they have together? Their eyes simply glow when one looks upon the other. It is very touching, very romantic," she said, her eyes taking on a sudden intensity, "and I want what they have for myself."

"Very well"—Julie sighed and pushed up her spectacles—"but if you must marry, why must you be in such a hurry?"

Griselda splayed her long fingers over her chest. "I am old, dearest. We must face facts, and the most unavoidable one of those is that I have precious little life left to dominate or spoil."

Julie looked away. "You may have another thirty years."

"And I may not." Griselda laid a warm hand on Julie's shoulder. "I *most likely* do not. Dear one, if I die next week, I wish to die a woman in love, and not just a woman who *is* loved. There is a difference."

There was nothing Julie could say to refute the argument. But there was still the matter of the medallions. "Why the medallions? Why not make your own choice?"

Griselda fiddled with her sleeve. "You have seen for yourself that each of the dozen loves me."

"Indeed," Julie said.

Men clung to Griselda Warring like the mists clung to the hills. In London, in Bath, in Bristol, in Brighton, she was always surrounded by an adoring cloud of masculine admirers. Her favorite dozen was only one of several dozens.

"I have chosen the dozen well, have I not?"

Julie had to concede it was so. Their adoration of Griselda had nothing to do with her wealth. Every one of the dozen ensconced at Alderley Manor were comfortably placed and not at all with pockets to let. They had each lived long and productive lives. It was Griselda they sought, not her fortune. "I will allow you could not find a more ardent group of admirers," she said.

Griselda smiled. "So you see? If I choose one among them, hearts will be broken, but if the love charms choose, none can feel forsaken or rejected."

Julie nodded. Griselda's argument was unassailable.

"Was there anything else, dear?" Griselda asked. "I must get back to my salon and finish a letter to my mantua-maker before luncheon. We are to meet at the inn on Wednesday next for the final fitting of my bridal gown." She clapped her hands together. "Robin's-egg colored satin, yards and yards of it. Delicious!"

She winked and sailed from the room, her slender form passing through patches of sunlight filtering through the windows and leaving behind swirling motes of dust in her wake.

Julie's insides swirled, too.

She sat perfectly still, attempting to sort out her thoughts and feelings, but it was no use. "Griselda—married?" She shook her head. "It is no wonder I can make no sense of it, for it is not sensible in the least.

"Even if marriage is the thing, using those ridiculous wedding charms to choose one's husband is not." *Fate will choose wisely for me,* Griselda's words echoed in Julie's head.

She scoffed. "Well," she muttered, "fate certainly did not choose so very wisely for me, now did it?" No, and there was no reason to think it could be trusted to choose wisely for Griselda, either.

Julie wandered to the window and stood thinking and watching the sky, where storm clouds were gathering, their turbulence a perfect mirror for the turmoil in her soul. If Griselda was determined to wed, there was nothing Julie could do about that, but there must be some way to convince Griselda to give up that medallion madness.

Julie didn't believe in that wedding charm nonsense for a second, and she couldn't let Griselda leave such an important decision up to what amounted to nothing outside random chance. She had to do something.

She stood thinking long enough for the clouds to gather and the rain to begin falling, but no solution came to her. She knew Lady Griselda well. For all the older woman's innate gentleness and kindness of spirit, she was also quite the most stubborn person Julie had ever known. If she believed she was right about something, there was no convincing her otherwise.

It was no use attempting to talk her out of using the medallions to make her choice. No, the medallions themselves would have to convince Lady Griselda of that.

Julie would just have to see they did.

Nine

Julie quivered with dread throughout supper that night. As always, she sat at table with the rest of the Alderley guests, but rather than conversing pleasantly as usual, she remained uncharacteristically quiet and kept a watchful eye on the steady stream of domestic traffic passing between the dining room and the kitchen, her eyes darting to each serving platter and dish as it was brought into the room.

Christopher noticed.

When the servants found out he'd quit the position of butler after only a day, there had been a minor revolt. They'd convinced him to try again. He wasn't faring too badly tonight, either. Fortunately, the only thing a butler did at supper was keep watch over the other servants and decant the wine, and though he was inept at most other household duties, he could remove a cork as deftly as anyone, and he was a virtuoso at organizing people.

He was also useful for keeping Sir Basil's ladies in line. The eccentric old gentleman always insisted his companions "dine" with him. They usually wandered variously about the room, lying about their master's feet or sniffing ankles under the table. But this time Christopher kept the lot of them at one end of the room—a relief, even to Sir Basil, it seemed.

Christopher stood at that end of the room for most of the long meal, listening and watching.

It seemed to Julie he hung upon every word, almost pitifully eager to observe. He was gathering information, she knew, re-educating himself—though what he could learn from a room full of besotted old gentlemen, one flighty spinster, and a newlywed old couple still behaving like mooncalves was doubtful.

It was no matter. He seemed to be focusing mostly on her anyway. He'd thrown her several questioning looks early on, before she'd made the attempt to be a little less conspicuous in her perusal of the serving dishes as they were brought to table.

It wouldn't be long now. The lemon tarts would be next, she was almost sure. Her heart beat a little faster. She wasn't quite sure how she was going to do what she knew had to be done.

She'd tried to sabotage Griselda's plan all day, but she'd been frustrated at every turn. The tarts hadn't been left alone for a second since Griselda made them. Cook hadn't even taken a nap that day, in spite of the heat and the humid air. It was most annoying— and frightening. Her mouth went dry as she waited for the tarts to be brought forth, and down in her lap, her fingers twisted the napkin mercilessly.

Christopher caught her gaze. A question appeared on his face. *What is it?* he mouthed and tilted his wildly blond-crowned head slightly to one side.

She looked away, pretending not to have seen.

Seconds ticked by and the contented banter at the table ceased as everyone listened to Mr. Percival Drake tell an amusing story about his recent trip to Cornwall. Julie tried to look fascinated.

And then the lemon tarts appeared. Sixteen plates on two large and heavy silver platters. Christopher was carrying one of them, and Mr. Biggs had been conscripted into carrying the other.

"And now, gentlemen," Griselda's voice rang out like a happy silver bell from the end of the table, "I have for you a special treat, lemon tarts I made myself."

It was so unusual for a lady to cook that some of them disavowed knowledge of where the kitchen was located in their own houses. But Griselda obviously did not heed such conventions. Her eyes were shining, her porcelain cheeks becomingly flushed. Her excitement and anticipation was well-nigh palpable, as plain to see as the enormous crystal chandelier hanging over the table.

The dozen noticed. To a man, they nearly fell over themselves to convey their own eager anticipation of a bite—a taste, the merest morsel!—of Griselda's delectable lemon tart.

Mr. Biggs approached with Christopher close on his heels, the platters balanced high in the air. Though they were strong, they were neither of them vastly accomplished serving men, and the platters swayed precariously.

Julie offered a fervent prayer they would drop the trays, but they did not. And then, as the two came abreast of Julie's chair, it became obvious they would reach their objective. The tarts would be served, and the supper would become Griselda's engagement party. Julie's heart threatened to beat its way out of her chest.

There was only one thing to do.

Pretending to do so by accident, she knocked a Cornish hen onto the floor beside her chair. Instantly, all seven of Sir Basil's ladies sprinted for it, as she knew they would, and Chris and Mr. Biggs were

surrounded by a swirling, barking, growling, whining, wriggling, tugging sea of dog. And then,
slipping her foot under the edge of a heavy woolen
carpet, she flipped it up, right in Christopher's path.

He stumbled, his tray tilted, and then, seemingly
in slow motion, the plates of tarts slid from the tray
and rained down onto Mr. Biggs's feet. The big man
stepped squarely onto one gelatinous plate and
slipped, falling with an audible thud onto his considerable backside, his own load of tarts cascading
down on top of him.

"Oh, my heavens!" Griselda cried. "Mr. Biggs! Mr.
Christopher! Are you hurt?"

"'M fine, mum," the beefy man said. One of the
plates had struck him on the face. With one large
finger, he wiped the gooey obstruction from his eye
and popped it into his mouth. "Mmm!" He didn't
look in the least unhappy for the turn of events.

Griselda chuckled. "And you, Mr. Christopher?"

Julie looked at Christopher, who was still standing.
"I am unhurt," he told Griselda, "though I am afraid
I have ruined your tarts."

"It is my fault," Griselda responded. "I should not
have allowed you to serve. Those trays are heavy, and
you are still not quite steady on your feet."

Griselda heaved a little sigh, but then her optimism took over. "I will enjoy making another sort of
tart on the morrow." She winked at Julie and, de-
claring supper to be finished, shepherded the
company to the drawing room for a game of twenty
questions.

Julie touched Lady Griselda's shoulder. "I will be
there in a moment." She dropped her voice to a
whisper. "The mull should be cleaned up before Mr.
Biggs finds the you-know-what."

"Oh, but surely someone else can—"

Julie shook her head. "Cook's rheumatism was bothering her today, and Mr. Christopher is unsteady, as you say."

Griselda nodded and smiled warmly. "Sweet, as always." She swept off and into the drawing room.

Julie turned around and nearly bashed straight into Christopher, who was standing in the midst of the ruined lemon tarts with his arms crossed over his chest in an unmistakable gesture of anger.

"Sweet?" he said. "That is hardly the word I would use."

Julie winced. *He knows.*

She gave a warning glance at Mr. Biggs, who was happily gobbling up a lemon tart, realizing with a thrill of alarm that he might accidentally eat one or both of the charms, but the feeling subsided instantly. If he did eat them, her bit of a rub would be solved. Griselda would have to make her own choice. She smiled and relaxed, sinking down onto a chair to watch.

Christopher growled. "In a pig's eye!" Scooping up the enormous joint of beef from the table, he thrust it at Mr. Biggs, who goggled. "Take it," Christopher said. The joint was only half eaten. It was an enormous amount of meat, even for Mr. Biggs, who didn't wait around long enough for the new butler to change his mind. He and the joint of meat disappeared in a flash, leaving Christopher and Julie alone in the dining room.

He rounded on her. "How dare you?"

There was no use denying what she'd done. It was obvious that he knew. "I know how things must look. I did not mean to—that is to say I. . . ." She faltered.

"You had no right," he said, his voice cutting

through the air like a rapier and vibrating with anger, and she drew back from him as though she'd been struck. "She is a grown woman," he said. "You argue she should not be controlled, and yet here you are controlling her."

"You were listening!" Outrage surged within her only to be supplanted by a cold fear that slid down her back. Just how much of Julie's conversation with Griselda had he overheard?

"Did you listen to the entire conversation—or only the parts that particularly interested you?" she asked, trying to sound merely sarcastic rather than afraid.

"I arrived somewhere in the middle and stayed until the end," he said.

"Somewhere near the middle!" she said sharply.

"Worried?" he asked. "Afraid I might have over-heard something about you, perhaps?"

She did not bother to deny it. "What is the first thing you heard?"

"I chanced by when you asked, *What changed your mind?* and Lady Griselda spoke of the love of the Robertsons."

She resisted an urge to sigh and close her eyes. He had not heard the parts about her.

"I froze in my tracks," he went on. "Could you not hear the longing in her voice, Julie? I was entranced. That is why I listened. I could not help myself."

"Still, you had no right!"

"Indeed, and that makes us even," he said, "for you have no right to interfere with her medallions. We are equally guilty."

He was right, of course.

Kneeling, he began to sift through the ruined

tarts with his bare fingers. "Are you going to help me?" he asked. "Or must I do this myself?"

"Can you not simply throw the lot of them away?" she asked sourly, crouching beside him.

He stopped moving. "Would you really deceive her like that?"

"I would do whatever I could to ensure her happiness."

"Two wrongs cannot make a right," he said.

"Neither can two wrongs make a love match," she said. "My mistress must allow her heart to choose, not some lump of cold metal."

"Your mistress may not have time to let her heart choose. Would you deprive her of any chance of experiencing the joy of marriage?"

His eyes had taken on an almost fierce intensity, and Julie trembled.

"What do you know of marriage?" she asked.

He shook his head. "Nothing. You know that."

"I wonder. . . ." she murmured.

"What do you mean?"

The lemon tarts lay forgotten between them.

"You speak of marriage with near reverence. I wonder if you *are* married."

"I do not know. I could also be a widower," he said, his voice calming suddenly, "or the son of a couple long and happily married. It is pointless to speculate."

At once, he turned his hands back to the lemon tart-littered plates, but Julie had the feeling his mind was not similarly engaged.

They worked together, clearing away the mess quickly and finding both of the charms. Julie washed them, and Christopher's eyes followed her as she

120 Melynda Beth Skinner

placed them on a shelf behind the salt. She could see the suspicion in his eyes.

"I will tell her where they are," she said.

Instantly suspicion was replaced with an expression of approval. "I am glad," he said.

Yes, she thought, *and I am a deceiver.* For, though she did intend to tell Griselda where the charms were, she did not intend to allow her to use them. Julie would find a way to sabotage the dessert again tomorrow. It was the right thing to do, even if it were not the above-board thing to do.

Her only misgiving was that she would have to face Christopher afterward, for he would certainly know who was responsible.

Ten

The day dawned bright and clear. Chris had awakened just before first light and set out for the brook. There was some truth to Griselda's assertion that he was still a little unsteady. He didn't quite trust himself to carry boiling water upstairs again, and yet he needed a proper bath rather desperately.

He crossed the quiet meadow and slipped through the wood, unaccompanied by Sir Basil's ladies for once, and reached the brook just as shafts of rosy light from the rising sun colored the sky. As he took off his borrowed clothing, he wondered not for the first time at the doctor's generosity in lending the garments. And then he paused at the water's edge to wonder at his own incredulity. It seemed he was always questioning others' motives. What sort of man was he? What sort of life had he led before coming here? Had he been surrounded with untrustworthy people? Is that why he expected everyone to be unkind?

Unwrapping his hand, he examined his odd-shaped burn, and then, leaving his spectacles, soiled clothing, spare shirt, and a towel on top of a flat rock, he submerged himself in the cold water and thought of Julie. He still didn't have her figured out. One moment she was spending time she did not have on helping a perfect stranger feel more at ease, and the next she was attempting to deprive an old woman of marriage.

And then there was the fact that she'd clearly been afraid when she'd realized he'd eavesdropped on her conversation with Griselda.

"What in hell was that about?" he wondered aloud. There was something about her, some secret, she did not want him to know.

He struck out against the current, swimming upstream a good distance before subsiding and floating back to his starting place. He just did not understand. How could she be so kind one moment and so heartless the next?

It did not make sense. She was either one or the other, heartless or kind. She could not be both.

He ducked his head under the water to rid himself of one sticky blob of lemon custard he had missed last night. Scrubbing his hair briskly with his fingers, he remembered the desperation in Julie's voice as she'd tried to convince her mistress not to wed. He'd listened from just outside the door of the library, knowing it was all out to do so but unable to stop himself. He *needed* to eavesdrop. It could gain him intelligence he might need to keep his position at Alderley. He could not feel contrite for such behavior. If he were turned away, he would have nowhere to go. No shelter, no food, and no way to procure employment. He would have no history and no references—not that he had any skills to offer a prospective employer anyway, for it seemed he was good for little but cavorting with Sir Basil's mutts and decanting wine. If he were turned away from Alderley Manor he would likely starve.

But that is not what worried him most.

Were he turned from Alderley Manor, he would be leaving behind the only people he knew. Meager as those relationships were, they were the only connections he had to anyone, and he recognized in himself a desperate desire to cling to them.

Where else would he find a group that would accept him?

Even when he had filled the house with smoke and deprived everyone of light, no one had looked askance. In that house of misfits, Christopher Christopher, the man with no past, fit right in.

Thank God he had the advantage of being reasonably intelligent and educated. If they would but tolerate his ineptitude for a short while, he might learn to be a proper butler and perhaps make a life for himself there in Alderley.

Though he told himself such thoughts were simply the natural result of wishing to avoid wandering the country lanes of England alone and cold, stealing eggs and apples and pies from windowsills and never knowing who he really was, another thought tore at the frayed edges of his consciousness—the thought that if he left Alderley Village, he would never see Julie Williams again.

He couldn't help thinking of the future. It had occupied most of his thought since he had awakened in this unfamiliar place. If his memory never returned, he'd have to settle somewhere, take up some occupation, marry some lady or other. . . .

A liquid image of himself standing next to a woman and swearing undying love flowed sinuously into his mind. Like a man dying of thirst, he drank.

"Married," he murmured. What would that be like? A sudden ache of longing seized him, sharp and bitter. The image swirled, resolved. He felt dizzy.

This time, the woman standing beside him was Julie Williams.

Ridiculous. He hardly knew her.

"What am I, some love-struck mooncalf who falls in love with the first pretty face he sees?"

Of course not. He was a man full grown and certainly not a man in love. And yet who else was he to marry if he stayed in this place? Alderley Village was small, and Julie Williams might be his only choice.

He swept his wet hair back away from his face with one hand. "There are worse fates," he said.

Climbing onto the bank, he strode to the rock and dried himself. Though it was August, the morning air was cool. It chilled his damp hair and cleared his brain. As he dressed to a symphony of awakening birdsong and rebandaged his hand, he felt alive and eager for what the day would bring.

Fortunately, the boots the doctor had lent him fit reasonably well. His burns were healing nicely, and they pained him less this morning. He pulled on a clean pair of stockings and the boots and struck out across the meadow toward the long, sloping road winding down the hill to Alderley Village, the same road he and Julie walked the morning before. She had exclaimed in delight over a luxuriant patch of forget-me-nots they'd seen there, and he wished to pick some for her chamber.

He'd been walking a few minutes and had the forget-me-not patch in sight when he heard a rider approach behind him.

"Hullo! You there!" the man hailed him.

Chris held up his bandaged hand in greeting, and the man pulled his horse to a stop. "Good day to you, sir," Chris said. "A fine morning, is it not?"

The man ignored the question and gestured into

the distance. "Is that Alderley House?" He looked as though he'd been riding all night. His clothes were dusty and his horse was flecked with foam. Without knowing quite why, Chris decided he didn't like the look of the stranger. He placed one hand casually atop a rock wall. "Chris Christopher at your service," he said, deliberately ignoring the man's question just as the man had done to him. "Are you in a hurry?"

A look of alarm passed over the man's features, but he mastered himself right away. "No . . . no. I just like a good hard morning ride is all. Thought I'd see the sights. Is that Alderley House yonder?"

Chris hesitated. He didn't want to disclose the location of the manor. Something deep inside warned him the man could not be trusted, but the location of Alderley Manor was hardly a secret. If Chris didn't affirm its location for the stranger, the man would find out soon enough from the next person he came upon.

Chris nodded toward where the stranger was pointing. The first rays of the sun were just warming Alderley Manor's dove-gray stone, and the house crowned the hill in a blush of pink.

"You did not tell me your name," Chris said.

"Cooper," the man answered. "Edward Cooper."

Chris held out his hand. Mr. Cooper looked down at it but hesitated a fraction of a second before extending his own. Chris held his face carefully impassive. The man's grip was quite strong, and he was dressed in the clothes of a workingman, but his hands were neatly manicured and free of calluses.

"New to the neighborhood?" Chris asked.

Mr. Cooper—if that was the man's name, which Chris now doubted—nodded. "Was passing through the area. Decided to stop, rest awhile. Pretty country you have here. Nice houses. They say Alderley House is the best hereabout." Once more he gestured toward the hill. "That it up there?"

Too single-minded, Chris decided. He liked the stranger less and less. "Though I too am a newcomer," he said, unable to keep a certain stiffness from his voice, "I believe I can say with fair authority the place is called Alderley *Manor.*"

The man's eyes flicked once more to the top of the hill. "Alderley Manor," he repeated. "You can be sure I will not forget." He gave a nod, turned his horse around without another word, and headed back the way he'd come.

Too slow.

Mr. Edward Cooper was not out for a good hard ride as he'd said. Neither was he out to see the sights. If he had been, he'd have continued on his way. He'd have had a closer look at Alderley Manor.

No, that man wanted something and wouldn't care how he got it.

Chris had no memories and hence no experience upon which to base such an assessment, but he knew it was accurate. Knew it down deep in his soul. The stranger was amoral at best, evil at worst. One thing for sure, he wasn't a common traveler. He was a thief—or worse. Chris would wager his spectacles the man was no common thief, either. Common thieves didn't care about the names of the houses they plundered. This one had a specific interest in Alderley Manor.

It wasn't difficult to guess why; there were a dozen reasons—a baker's dozen, counting Mrs. Ophelia Robertson. Where the rich traveled, thieves were no distance behind.

Making quick work of gathering flowers for Julie,

Chris hopped over the stone wall and struck out across the wide, green meadow, a shortcut toward Alderley Manor. Unlike the lane, the meadow afforded no shade, and by the time he was halfway up the hill he was winded and even a little dizzy, but he kept going. Even though Mr. Cooper had headed in the opposite direction, Chris hurried. Thieves often had accomplices, and the men at Alderley Manor should be alerted right away.

Julie was just returning from milking and egg-gathering as he crested the hill from the southeast. His boots and the bottom third of his breeches were wet from having brushed against the high, dewy meadow grass.

She waited for him on the doorstep.

He forced a smile and waved. He hadn't decided whether to tell the women at Alderley what he'd learned or not.

"Good morning, Christopher!" she called.

"You are up early."

"Always," she nodded. She looked busy, yet relaxed and happy, and she was fetchingly dressed in a deep yellow cotton frock and a cream colored shawl. "Why did you not keep to the lane?" she asked as he approached, nodding toward his breeches. "The grass is too wet this time of the—oh, la! What is wrong?"

Astonishment streaked through him. "Why do you think something is wrong?"

"You are walking too briskly and your face is . . . a little drawn, perhaps. I do not know really. Am I right?"

"You are." He nodded.

"Well?" she prompted. "Are you going to tell me about it?"

"Truth to tell," he said, "I had not decided."

"Too late," she said with a triumphant grin. "Now you have no choice."

"Indeed," Chris said, mirroring her smile.

Accompanying her to the kitchen, he told her of his encounter with the stranger, Mr. Cooper.

"I know no one by that name near here."

"He said he was only passing through," Chris told her.

She raised one delicate brown eyebrow. "I will wager he was telling the truth about that much, but I suspect he plans to make an unannounced stop or two before he leaves the neighborhood."

"My thoughts exactly," Chris said.

Then, they both spoke at once: "I shall tell the—" "I will inform the—"

They stopped. "The servants?" Julie asked.

Chris nodded. "The men, at least. No need to worry the women."

Inexplicably, she frowned. "And why not?" she said archly. "I believe they have a right to know."

"They are ladies."

"And?"

"And it is not their duty to protect home and hearth. That is the men's responsibility."

"And so you would pretend there is nothing wrong, keep the women in the dark, deprive them of the truth?"

"I would not put it that way."

"Just how would you put it, Mr. Christopher?"

"Botheration! There it is again. *Mr.* Christopher. I have managed to prick your temper again, and I have no idea how."

"Shall I enlighten you?"

"Yes, please do—right after you accept my sincere apology."

Her eyebrows came together and she tilted her head to one side. "You do not even know what you did wrong."

"Ah, but you seem to think I've done something dreadful. I will trust you—and therefore I apologize."

A wry smile slid over her face, and she gave him a sideways look. "Honey-tongued knave."

He bowed. "At your service, my captain."

She laughed. "Go on with you!"

Chris-as-butler called the staff together formally. The kitchen was filled with curious faces, faces that turned grim, angry, resolute, or worried as he told them of his suspicions concerning Edward Cooper.

A watch list was agreed upon. At least two men would keep watch at all times, day and night, and Cook promised to brew strong coffee before she retired.

When Chris dismissed the servants, he glanced at Julie.

"Thank you for trusting us," she said. Her eyes were shining, and he knew she spoke of the women.

He nodded. "Can you use an extra pair of hands?"

He helped her pour the milk into several crocks, carried water, cleaned the ashes from the oven and fireplace, and cracked open several dozen eggs while she set about helping Cook make breakfast. As he worked, he watched her surreptitiously extract several pieces of stray eggshell from the pan on the stove, though she said not one word about it.

She was kind, and he was terribly grateful.

They worked companionably side by side throughout the morning, pausing only to seek *The Morning*

Post. It had been delivered that morning as they worked unawares, and Sir Basil had read it, as before. This time, however, he'd misplaced it—"though there was nothing of interest to you there, my boy," Sir Basil assured him. "So sorry."

Nothing of interest. No pleas for the safe return of a missing loved one. It had been three days. Chris was grimly aware that if anyone cared for him, loved him, they would have contacted the papers by then. Chances were he was as alone in his former life as he was in this one.

Bitterly disappointed, he tried not to show it, but somehow Julie knew.

Laying one soft hand lightly upon his shoulder, she squeezed. "I am sorry, Christopher."

The day passed in a blur of activity. Even with the addition of Christopher's help, there was too much to do. While Lady Griselda's favorite dozen and the Robertsons were not odious houseguests by any means, they were still fourteen people who needed to be fed and entertained. And then there were their servants, valets, coachmen, and a lady's maid who needed food, too. The demand upon Cook was too much. Up at ten o' the clock, she was napping by noon. Julie had no time for anything but cooking.

Thank goodness for Christopher!

In between dishes, she instructed him on what needed to be done elsewhere. Though he was terribly unskilled at the most simple tasks, he was intelligent and quick-minded, and it seemed he took pleasure in helping as best he could.

Somewhere around the hour of two, Ophelia Robertson invaded the kitchen.

She was a handsome woman, not fragile and beautiful like Griselda, but she had clever blue eyes and moved quickly. She was wont to use sweeping gestures, speak kindly if a little flamboyantly—and she dressed even more flamboyantly, favoring spangles, feathers, and brilliantly clashing shades of magenta and orange.

She was Griselda's dearest and oldest friend.

She was also Julie's friend, the only other person in the world besides Griselda who knew Julie's true identity, and she was the only person who knew that Julie was married. She had found Julie's husband for her, arranging everything, and Julie hadn't breathed a word of it to Griselda, for she hadn't wanted to worry the old dear or chance Griselda's attempting to dissuade her, and so she had married in secret.

Julie had come to Alderley Manor at Mrs. Robertson's insistence. Griselda needed a companion, she had said, and that was that. Though Griselda had put up a token protest, Julie gathered, Mrs. Robertson would hear none of it, and an advertisement was placed into the paper forthwith. Julie had been the first person to answer it, and the only person interviewed. She'd worn a simple red gown and a white shawl embroidered with red pug dogs to the interview.

Griselda hired her on the spot, proclaiming the red pugs perfect. Fortunately, as time went on, she'd been just as enthusiastic about the person wearing them—and Ophelia Robertson had been smug about the matter ever since.

"Dearling," Mrs. Robertson said in her direct way, "you need help. This"—she gestured about her, making it plain as a pikestaff she meant the house party—"is too much."

132   *Melynda Beth Skinner*

At that moment, Christopher came through the back door with the most brilliant smile on his face, dirt under his fingernails, and his expression full of pride. He'd been weeding the kitchen garden.

She made appreciative noises as she leaned out the window to inspect his work. "La, Christopher, I cannot believe it! How . . . how surprised I am!"

She didn't have the heart to tell him he'd pulled up half of the Brussels sprouts and every last carrot. He left looking for all the world like a lad who had just said, "Look at me, Mama!"

"No carrots for Christmas," Mrs. Robertson remarked when he'd gone.

"Not a one," Julie sighed.

"My girl, I fear you will not survive. You need help," she repeated. "You should have engaged extra servants from the village."

"I cannot," Julie said. "It is harvest time."

"I did not think you would agree, which is why I have sent for my Town servants. They should arrive in a few hours—sixteen of them."

"Sixteen! Where shall I put them all?"

"The garrets, of course—where proper servants belong."

Mrs. Robertson didn't quite approve of her friend's familiarity with the servants, but since she had married one, she had little margin to pass judgement.

"The garrets have not been lived in for several years," Julie said. "They are not ready to accommodate your staff."

"My staff will see to their own accommodations. No need to fret, you will see. My butler Bendleson is quite capable of producing order from any sort of chaos." She chuckled. "I have put him to the test often enough." She turned and whisked through the door, calling over her shoulder, "He can probably even give your new butler a lesson or two."

Julie laughed. "Your tiger could probably give our new butler a lesson or two."

Ophelia turned and dimpled. "Indeed—though your Mr. Christopher is quite nice to look at, is he not? Very decorative." She winked and whirled off in the direction of the parlor, where a fierce card game had raged all morning.

Julie stared after her, amused. Mrs. Robertson was right. Christopher was nice to look at. That had taken Julie by surprise. He looked vastly different now from when he'd first arrived. Over the last two days, the evidence of the blows his face sustained had subsided. With clean clothes, a bath, and all his sails furled, he was more than just nice to look at. He was a diamond—though she supposed most might see him as a diamond-in-the-rough. His too-long blond hair would never be tamed and, although he had neatly trimmed his long sideburns, they too gave him a rakish, pirate-like air, matching blue eyes that sparkled with roguish mischief. But he didn't need a cut-and-polish, she thought. It would ruin his charm.

Realizing she was woolgathering, she pulled her mind back to the problem at hand.

Though it chafed her independent spirit to admit it—even to herself—she really did need help. Even two years ago, the Alderley staff might have been able to handle the house party by themselves with her help, but now . . . not even Christopher's help was enough.

In spite of the workload, Julie had a lovely afternoon. It was now common knowledge Lady Griselda had decided to marry, and the servants could not have been happier for her. Even with everyone as overworked as they were, the atmosphere had turned merry.

Julie was still worried, knowing supper—and another dessert—was coming, but it was difficult not to feel cheerful among the whistling, humming, smiling staff. Their optimism was infectious.

Julie would find a way to lead Lady Griselda to make her own choice, and that was that.

So it was, that when she walked into the kitchen for a quick cup of tea and found Christopher there helping Cook, she sang out, "Hullo, Christopher! Lovely day, is it not?"

He frowned and, wrinkling his nose, looked down at the worktable. "For everyone else, perhaps."

He was up to his elbows in eels.

She beamed a wry smile at him. "Helping Cook, I see. Where is she?"

"Down at the ice house with Mr. Wells and Mr. Sully."

Julie poured some boiling water into the teapot and leaned against the windowsill. Slipping one shoe off, she flexed her foot against the hard stone floor of the kitchen.

"Why not sit down for a moment or two?" he asked. "I daresay the house will not crumble before your tea brews."

"I do not know . . . I like my tea strong and sweet. It takes an extra minute in the brewing. Are you sure the house will not fall over in that time?"

"No," he said with a grin.

She chuckled and sat. "Ah . . ." She sighed. "I hadn't realized how much my feet hurt."

"Mmm," he grunted, his nose wrinkling once again. He was skinning and gutting the eels, a task

Julie knew pained Cook's hands when the rheumatism struck. By the look, the task pained Christopher as well—though for an entirely different reason. The poor man was trying to clean the fish using only two fingers on each hand. She bit her lip to keep herself from laughing.

"Have you remembered anything else of your past?" she asked by way of distraction, though which of them needed distraction more was debatable.

"Yes," he said. "I hate eels."

She did laugh then. "No . . . seriously."

"I am being serious. I hate eels. Live eels, dead eels, fresh eels, cleaned eels, cooked eels. Stewed, sautéed, fried, dried, broiled, or baked. I detest the taste of them, the smell of them, the look of them, and most especially the feel of them." He screwed up his face and looked at his slimy hands with distaste. "There is not enough water in the ocean to rid me of this smell."

At that moment, Cook scurried back into the kitchen, clucking warnings like a worried hen to the puffing Sully and Wells, who were carrying an enormous block of ice. Julie grimaced. Undaunted by last night's lemon tart disaster, Lady Griselda planned to make a cream and raspberry shaved ice for that night's dessert.

"Look at you, now, my little lost puppy!" Cook patted Christopher in approval. "A champion eel peeler you be!"

"Thank you," Chris said quietly without a word of complaint or even so much as a curled lip.

Lost puppy? Julie silently mouthed.

Christopher shrugged, mirth dancing about his blue-green eyes.

He kept his face otherwise impassive and continued

skinning and gutting the eels as though he were doing nothing more odious than peeling apples. He was obviously sparing Cook's feelings.

When he looked up a few moments later, Julie told him with a soft smile how grateful she was.

She savored the last sip of her tea and then washed and dried her dishes. They belonged in the empty spot on a special shelf above the oven. Everyone who lived at Alderley Manor had his own set—even Lady Griselda, who loved to sit by the kitchen fire in the morning drinking chocolate and reading. And, as odd as she knew it must be, everyone took care of his own dishes, washing and drying them as needed—even Lady Griselda, who insisted on being treated no differently in that respect. As Julie replaced her cup and saucer on the shelf, it occurred to her it might make poor Christopher feel more welcome if he had a set of dishes, too.

She smiled and turned to leave. "I will return before long."

But she wasn't back soon at all. Halfway down the hall, Sir Basil approached, looking terribly worried.

"Oh, Miss Williams, have you seen Mr. Christopher? I need—she needs, rather—no . . . no, we need him. But, dear me, what if Mr. Christopher cannot help?" He laid one hand on her arm and bustled off, calling over his shoulder, "You had best send for the doctor!"

Eleven

"The doctor!" Julie scurried to catch up to him. "Who is ill?"

"Lady Cowper!" Sir Basil said, his eyes full of fear. "My fuzzy little white lamb. Her human counterpart was Emily Lamb, you know, before she married Lord Cowper. Oh, Miss Williams, she is such a friendly thing. Spends every night sleeping at my feet, the darling. I do not know what I should do without her."

"Without whom?" Mrs. Robertson demanded imperiously, coming down the hall with Griselda, arm-in-arm. The two fell into step behind Sir Basil and Julie.

"Lady Cowper," Sir Basil answered over his shoulder. "Never met a gentleman she did not like—or a lady for that matter."

"Lady Cowper?" Ophelia exclaimed.

"She sleeps with me every night—a great comfort when it is cold."

Julie glanced back at Ophelia, whose eyes had grown as big and round as the wheels of the Prince Regent's high-perch phaeton.

"Why, Sir Basil," Ophelia cried, "either you have truly gone mad at last, or you are an insufferable scapegrace! The Countess Cowper is a lady—in every sense of the word."

Griselda laughed, the sound's echoing trill bouncing off the high walls of the long hallway. "He is not speaking of *the* lady, my friend, but of *his* lady."

But Ophelia's face was still a confused cluster of storm clouds—until they rounded the corner into the library, where Lady Cowper lay on an enormous Turkish carpet under a draped table, panting and shifting nervously. "Ohh," Ophelia said.

Julie knelt there, crooning softly, and ran her hands experimentally over the dog's body.

"I do not think the doctor can be of much help, Sir Basil."

"W-what is she suffering from? Go on—I can take it. I fought in America, you know."

"She suffers from"—Julie coughed delicately— "ah . . . rather too much friendliness."

Sir Basil looked befuddled.

"She is in the family way," Julie said, "and I suspect you shall soon be the proud owner of several more dogs, by the feel of her."

"Well, bless me!" Sir Basil cried. "I had no notion, what with her all fluffy like that. I did think she was a little fatter than usual, but I attributed it to the time of year—she has a habit of eating too much during the Season, you see, and I thought she had just—" He lowered his voice to a whisper and shielded his mouth from view of Lady Cowper. "I thought she had just got a little too plump, as she always does." He got down on his hands and knees and reached under the table to pat the round ball of white fluff. "Everything will be fine, little lamb, you will see. I am certain Doctor Brown will soon set the lot to rights."

Julie turned her head to hide her grin as she imagined the doctor's face when he rushed to Alderley Manor only to discover his patient was a poodle with an interesting condition. How she would laugh!

But the humor of the situation evaporated as she realized she would likely be the one to fetch him, the one to tell him he was being summoned to play midwife to a poodle—and he would not be amused.

"Doctor Brown has little experience with this sort of thing," she said, backing out from under the table and standing. Her eyes caught the time on the mantel clock. *Three-thirty!* She had to get back to the menus and the accounts or there would soon be no meals.

"Oh," Sir Basil said. "Oh. Yes, yes, of course a lady would be better for this sort of thing. Just so." He coughed nervously. "Under the circumstances." He coughed again. "I am sure you will do famously, my dear."

"Oh, but—" Julie shook her head.

"Now, now," Sir Basil said, patting her shoulder, "I am certain you are capable. A better choice than the doctor, I dare say. You are female, after all. Yes, I leave Lady Cowper in your good hands—yours and my kennel master's, of course." He nodded at Christopher, who was just entering the room. "If anything alarming happens, please do inform me—though we may be out taking the air later. Perhaps you could open the window and ring that big bell there." He pointed to the largest of Lady Griselda's bells, a massive and ornate silver affair Julie doubted she could pick up, let alone ring.

"But—"

"You both have our complete confidence," Griselda said with a soft smile and a wink.

The three older people left, discussing the quandary with which Basil would soon be faced in naming the pups.

"Almack's has only seven patronesses. Do you think they would object," he asked Griselda and Ophelia before they were quite out of Julie and Christopher's earshot, "if I named the pups after their children?"

When they'd truly gone, Christopher turned to Julie with a grin. "Do the real patronesses know Sir Basil's ladies are named after them?"

"I do not see how they can have missed it."

"I will wager they do not much like it."

Julie giggled. "I would not wager against you. Sir Basil hasn't been granted a subscription to Almack's in several years."

He chuckled and then looked down at Lady Cowper, who was still panting nervously under the table. "Well," he said, raking his fingers through his hair, "do you think she would feel more secure if I put her in a crate from the stables?"

Julie nodded. "Indeed. I know *I* would. That carpet was expensive."

He laughed again, a rich, resonant sound that seemed to come from deep inside him. Julie liked to hear him laugh.

His face was even less livid today, less swollen. His long sideburns and halo of dark blond curls framed a face more intriguing than handsome, his expression a mix of innocent wonder and weary cynicism. The combination was incongruent, and it begged questions. What was his past? How had he become the man he was—suspicious, yet trusting; wary, yet appetent; pensive, yet animated. He was a curious jumble of contradicting attitudes, and Julie wished she knew why. The answers were all in his past.

She wondered if Christopher would be about long

enough for her to begin to understand him. She hoped so.

No.

Mentally, she shook herself. What she hoped was that he would regain his memory and return to his proper place in life. That is what he needed. Her wishes did not matter.

"Well, then. I am off to the stable yard," he said.

He was gone for some time. Poor Lady Cowper got up and paced to the door as soon as he'd gone. Looking out the doorway, her ears flapped a time or two, and then she resumed pacing. It was only when Christopher returned that she settled back down again.

"I think she likes you," Julie said, watching him make a nest for Lady Cowper out of the wooden crate and an old blanket.

"We understand each other," he said, stroking Lady Cowper's head and ruffling her floppy ears. "After all, we are both Sir Basil's strays."

Julie opened her mouth to protest but closed it once more. "A denial sprang to my lips, but I confess I myself referred rather uncharitably to you as such on the night you arrived. One of Sir Basil's strays."

"Seeing as I was foxed, dirty, half-naked, and bleeding all over everything at the time,"—he threw her a wry smile—"you are forgiven."

"Would you care for a game of backgammon while we wait?" she asked.

"Only if you like to lose," he said, a merry challenge in his eye.

"Hmmph!" she returned. "We shall see."

He beat her four games to three, and they had just started an eighth when Cook bustled in carrying a small rag-wrapped parcel and a tray, which she set upon a table by the door. "There you are, Mr. Christopher! And Miss Julie too! I just heard the good news." She peered under the table. "Ooo, she looks peckish, doesn't she?" She unwrapped the parcel and handed a meaty ham bone to Christopher, who offered it to Lady Cowper.

The dog sniffed at it but looked away, untempted. "Ah, well," said Cook. "I know how it is. She'll be prime enough for it later, I dare say. Once she whelps her pups, she'll behave like she's been starved. Are you two hungry, as well?" She looked from Christopher to Julie.

"Starving." Julie grinned.

"Splendid. And you?" she asked Christopher.

"Famished."

She clapped her hands together and grinned. "Good, just good!" Retrieving the tray from the table near the door, she flipped off the cloth cover to reveal two very small bowls of soup.

Eel soup.

"My specialty," Cook beamed, handing a bowl to Christopher. "You shall have the first taste, since you're the one what cleaned the beasties. I hate skinning the things. Hurts my poor old knobby hands—and gives me the shivers," she confided, and then she shivered, just thinking about it.

Julie grasped her own bowl and stared with horrified fascination as Christopher took his spoon in hand. It was going to break Cook's heart when her new pet said nay to the eel soup. It really was her specialty—a delicious concoction of tender eel, port wine, mussels, and herbs legendary in the neighborhood. It was a source of considerable pride for her—and she clearly looked forward to the rapturous expression on her *lost puppy's* face when he tasted the soup.

Julie held her breath, hoping Christopher would find some gentle way to ease Cook's disappointment.

"Thank you," he said with a smile, and then he did something that made Julie's mouth drop open. He tasted the soup, rolled it around on his tongue, looking skyward, and then his eyes lit up. He dipped in again and filled his spoon to the brim, slurped the soup down, and then proceeded to clean the small bowl of the rest.

"Mmm!" he exclaimed. "Cookie, my dear, that was undeniably the best eel soup I have ever had in my life."

Cook blushed and batted at him. "Go on with you."

But before Christopher could issue any further false praise, Cook wheeled and headed for the door. "I'm that sorry it's such a little bowl," she said. "I didn't know if you'd like it, you see. I'll just go and fetch you a big bowl." She paused and looked back with a fond smile. "The biggest bowl I have."

"You are too kind," Christopher said.

Cook quit the room singing, and Christopher plunked down dejectedly on the floor near Lady Cowper.

"Oh, God." He groaned.

Julie looked down at Christopher with admiration and then moved to stand next to him. "*You* are too kind," she said quietly and touched him fleetingly on the shoulder. She would miss him when he regained his memory and left Alderley.

Before she could remove her hand, he captured

it in his. "Do you truly think I am kind?" he asked. "That would make me quite happy."

She took her hand from his and danced lightly away from him. "Of—of course." She picked up her soup bowl, the spoon clattering against the bottom, and her heart clattering against her ribs.

La! Had he just signaled an interest in her? Or was it like the morning after he'd come to them, when he'd said all that rubbish about how beautiful she was?

That was it. It was all just polite hums, pleasantries any young man might offer a young woman in similar circumstances.

Or was it?

Truth to tell, she didn't know. She hadn't ever been courted, after all. Even before she was truly marriageable, long before she could have any sort of come-out, her guardian, Uncle Elbert, had pushed her toward marrying a friend of his. The prospective groom was an odious man, simpering and lisping. It made her skin crawl to think of him even now.

They had set a wedding date before she was even asked.

No, she'd never had any experience with sincere flirtation.

Her hand tingled and felt warm where she and Christopher had touched, which was ridiculous. She was making too much of nothing, turning another polite compliment into evidence of a *tendre*.

She had to get hold of herself.

"I must go retrieve my ledgers and writing desk," she said, avoiding his eyes. "I will work while we wait. I fear there is little else we can do for our charge."

While she was gone, she made a detour into the dish closet, where all of the crockery, china, silver,

linens, and crystal were kept. Lady Griselda loved
such things, and she often purchased the odd piece
at a market fair or from a street vendor. The tall
shelves were full of cups and saucers and plates
and bowls of all shapes, sizes, and colors. Julie
stood and pondered for only a second or two before chuckling and climbing to the top shelf to
bring down a deep sea-green bowl, a wide blue
plate, and a large white saucer and cup with a handle in the shape of an eel. Carefully, she carried
the things to the kitchen, washed them and set
them on the long shelf in a place she cleared for
them, right between Mrs. Mapes's pink shepherdesses and lambs and Mr. Sully's plain whites.
Then she neatly pinned a card with Christopher's
name onto the shelf and returned to the library
with a smile.

In spite of all her earlier reasoning to the contrary,
her heart beat faster when she saw him there. He'd
pulled a wing chair over next to Lady Cowper's table,
and he watched the dog with a compassionate, concerned expression. He looked up as she entered,
though, and his expression changed. It grew warmer,
as though he were thinking of something pleasant.

Her heart pounded in her ears, and she followed
a straight course to one of the windows, where she
sat and tried quite unsuccessfully to keep her mind
on the figures in her ledger.

It wasn't long before Mrs. Robertson's servants
arrived, providing some welcome distraction. She
spent a busy half-hour showing the Robertson butler, Mr. Bendleson, the house and grounds, but
then she had very little to do and was obliged to return to the library, her stomach full of the
flutters—not that there was any reason for it. There

were no more fulsome glances or pressings of the hands. Christopher might as well have been a brother or a governess, for all the heat in his gaze.

She tried to tell herself she was relieved.

"Can eels kill rhododendrons?" he asked suddenly, interrupting her fifth attempt to total a column of numbers correctly.

"What?"

He pointed to a very large empty bowl on a tray near the door. "The window opens," he said with an apologetic shrug. "Thank God."

Julie laughed.

As Ophelia had promised, Mr. Bendleson was a marvel of efficiency. Somehow, the newcomers were all absorbed into the household without a ripple. Julie worried about the Alderley servants feeling inadequate—until she overheard one of the Robertson footmen asking Mr. Sully's advice on the proper care of horses and then walked into the kitchen to find the Robertson cook exclaiming over Cook's eel soup.

Bendleson's staff was suspiciously uninformed and her own staff happily eager to educate them. It was a ruse, Julie knew. Bendleson had obviously ordered his staff to defer to hers in an effort to ease the older group's embarrassment over needing help. But, as the day wore on, the smart young Town staff discovered they really did have a thing or two to learn after all. The Alderley servants had lived full, robust lives. They knew what was what—even if they couldn't always *remember* what was what.

Mrs. Robertson's staff were well-chosen, well-mannered, and well-trained. They were only too happy to put a polish on their skills with the help of the Alderley staff.

By suppertime, the house was humming along with the precision of clockwork, and there were three new puppies in the library—all male—named Brummel, Byron, and Bedford.

If not for the grim presence of the pots of fresh cream and raspberries, the cake of sugar, and the large block of ice all waiting ominously in the kitchen, Julie would have been completely happy.

Twelve

Supper that night was grander than it had been in years. Aided by the Robertson servants, Cook had turned out a feast worthy of Brighton Pavilion. From the wonderful eel soup and creamed haddock to the pigeon pie and the braised mutton, supper was elaborate and plentiful, but Julie didn't taste a bite of it. Her stomach was in knots, awaiting the arrival of the raspberry ice.

Unfortunately, she wasn't the only one watching for it. Christopher was awake on every suit. She knew he wouldn't allow her to trip him again—not that it mattered, for her plan for the raspberry ice didn't involve well-placed feet or a pack of yapping dogs.

When the little red china bowls containing the raspberry ice finally made an appearance, they were carried in on a tray by one of the experienced Robertson footmen, whom Christopher directed to walk on the side of the room opposite Julie. As the ruby-colored ice in the ruby-colored bowls was served, Julie met his gaze. He looked more satisfied than triumphant, she decided, and then his expression changed, became apologetic. Even though he didn't agree with her, he was clearly empathetic.

She might have felt guilty about it, if she didn't know his empathy would change to anger quicker than a thunderclap after the flash, once she had gone through with her plan.

It was no matter. She was clearly in the right. Her motive was pure. She wasn't trying to keep Griselda from marrying, she was only compelling the older woman to make her own choice. There was nothing wrong with that.

Just as the first ice was set upon the table, Julie cried, "Oh, la, no!"

Every head turned her way—including Christopher's. Julie swallowed. "I have lost my ring," she said.

"Oh, dear, how perfectly dreadful!" Mrs. Robertson cried.

And Lady Griselda asked, "Which ring is it, my dear?"

Julie's plan was to answer *my ruby ring* and then pretend the ring had somehow ended up in the raspberry ice as she'd helped Cook that afternoon, but she was saved from the odious necessity of issuing a lie by none other than Sir Basil, who chose that moment to make a startling declaration.

"Bless me, but I dislike the color red," he interjected into the silence. He was staring down at his own waistcoat, which was a rich wine color.

Griselda's eyes grew round. Red was her favorite color, and she wore some shade of it more often than not. Even now, she was wearing a lovely silk gown of deepest crimson. Basil's admission clearly discomfited her.

"Makes me dyspeptic," he went on. "Always has. Do not know why I have abided it these fifty years. Well, no longer!" he said with a shrug and stood up. To the astonishment of the entire company, Sir Basil shrugged out of his coat and threw his waistcoat onto the fire, then put his coat back on. "Much better," he said on a sigh. "From this day on," he announced, "I will wear no red. Nor will I eat red food. Makes me dyspeptic," he repeated, wrinkling his nose at the silver tray of red ices on the hunt board. He looked around, seeming to notice for the first time that everyone was staring at him and coughing a little from the smoke of the burning cloth. "Eh? Go on, go on. Do not let me disturb your dessert. I am quite happy to do without."

The servants resumed serving, and Julie opened her mouth again to say her ring had been lost in the ice, but Mrs. Ophelia Robertson beat her to it.

"No!" Ophelia cried. "Do not eat that!" Reaching out, she snatched two dishes of ice from in front of the gentlemen next to her. "You might bite down on Miss Williams's ring!" Julie almost fell out of her chair, and Mrs. Robertson went on, "You *were* in the kitchen today, my dear, were you not?"

"Indeed," Julie replied.

"And she helped with the raspberries," Ophelia said. Beneath the table, Ophelia's slippered foot made swift contact with Julie's shin. "Correct?"

"Oh! Yes!" Julie said, nodding. "Yes, quite so."

Ophelia threw a speaking look at Griselda, her eyes widening and her eyebrows rising meaningfully.

"Oh!" Griselda cried. "Oh, I . . . ah . . . I am most—most dreadfully sorry," she stammered, her gaze glued to Ophelia's. "Ah . . . yes. Yes, Miss Williams's ring may be in the raspberry ice." Rising, Griselda rapidly removed the other two dishes of raspberry ice remaining on the table and whisked them off to the kitchen, calling over her shoulder that she would return shortly. Everyone was to sit and "have a nice little chat," while she brought out another dessert from the kitchen.

Most of the company looked bemused—all except Sir Basil, who seemed not to notice his hostess' strange behavior, and Christopher, who understood it all too well. He knew, just as Julie did, that Ophelia and Griselda's odd behavior was logical, strange as it seemed. The medallions couldn't work their magic unless every one of the dozen had a share of the ice.

Expecting their hostess to be away for a good while, the guests settled into the usual polite subjects— horses, London, golf, and the weather—while Julie excused herself and made for the kitchen.

If Griselda was making another dessert and she had two dishes of raspberry ice in her hands when she left, there was a remote possibility that she had both of the medallions, and Julie wasn't taking any chances. Excusing herself without bothering to offer a pretext, she rushed off to the kitchen, arriving just behind Griselda, who was terribly flustered.

"Red . . . red!" She muttered, placing a huge vase of white roses upon the kitchen table. Julie recognized them as the ones that had been in the drawing room, right up until supper was announced.

"How can he not like red?" Griselda went on muttering, pulling the roses out of the vase and tugging at their petals. "Everyone likes red!" She dismembered the flowers, making a fluffy mountain of fragrant white on the table. Quickly, she dampened the petals *en masse* with some warm cream and then rolled the lot in coarse sugar before plopping the sugared petals onto serving plates and sailing back toward the dining room with instructions to the servants to serve the concoction immediately. She hadn't even noticed Julie standing there.

The servants, Cook, and six of the Robertson staff

stood motionless and blinking at one end of the kitchen.

"Is she really going to serve them nobs nought but flowers for dessert, miss?" Cook asked.

Julie shrugged and followed her mistress back to the dining room, where the servants soon substituted the sugared rose petals for the raspberry ice.

A delighted Sir Basil happily munched away. "They are not red!" he said.

The rest of the dozen, along with the Robertsons and Julie, only pushed the things industriously about on their plates, giving the illusion—albeit a not very convincing one—that they were not abjectly declining the makeshift dessert.

But Griselda didn't seem to notice, for she was too busy talking with Basil and nibbling rose petals. The two of them wore sublime expressions, the Robertsons looked speculative, while, to a man, the dozen scowled.

Julie had a difficult time trying to keep from laughing—a task made all the more difficult when she saw Christopher was in the same predicament. His brown eyes danced with merriment, and he quickly busied himself with a bottle of wine—though not before glancing over at Julie with a covert wink.

Thirteen

Posted from Buxley-on-Isis:

That thing you seek, I know where it is. Come quick and bring what you promised me.

The next day was one of the loveliest Julie could remember.

With the Robertson servants about, there was nothing for her to do, and with Griselda's dozen about, she had all the companionship she needed. No one was ill, the weather was fine, and Julie spent the day at leisure, walking about the grounds, drawing pictures of the wildflowers, and playing her harp up on the high meadow, something at which she possessed no skill but which delighted her nonetheless.

Christopher joined her periodically, and, while she expected him to question her about last night's sabotage of the dessert, he remained silent, owing perhaps to the role of Ophelia in the event. Her own intentions were—just barely—beyond reproach.

Misusing the poor harp dreadfully, she taught him several lullabies, and he taught her several songs she'd never heard before but which were quite entertaining. They ended by mixing up the tunes and melding the words into ribald lullabies that had them clutching their sides with laughter. In this way, they spent several pleasant hours together—marred only by a report from Sir Basil of no news of mysterious disappearances in *The Morning Post.*

For a third time, there had been a mishap with the newspaper. Sir Basil had batted at a flying cinder, he said, and the paper had caught fire, a pronouncement that sent Chris and Julie into fits of merriment as soon as poor Sir Basil was out of hearing range. Much idle time was devoted to making up songs involving the destruction of newspapers, teaching Christopher to weave daisy chains—something he marveled at—and telling Christopher fairy stories, which he'd apparently never heard before. The day passed quickly.

Much too quickly.

The assembled company were playing charades in the drawing room when Christopher, shadowed by Bendleson, who was clearly tutoring the new Alderley butler, gave notice that supper was but a half hour away, and Julie realized in a panic that she didn't have any idea what Griselda had planned for dessert—or how she was going to attack it this time.

She needn't have worried.

Immediately, Griselda provided the needed intelligence, for she became all a-twitter over "the black currant tarts I have made today."

"I am certain they will be delicious, my dear lady," said one portly old gentleman wearing a powdered wig.

"They?" joked another, though Julie thought she detected a sharp edge under the velvet of his voice. "Planning to eat them all, are you?"

Griselda batted at the offender playfully with her fan, making it clear she did not believe his victim was a glutton, but she admonished the company nevertheless that there was only one tart for each of them. "One tart apiece, and please take care with them, as I want you all to have a taste."

Several gray heads bobbed their understanding, but old Baron Albury, his head as bald and white as the cliffs at Dover, piped up, *"We* shall be careful," he said—the unspoken corollary being that perhaps the servants would not.

Albury laughed and grinned at his own cleverness until he noticed Griselda staring at him. She wasn't smiling. He hung his head. "It—it was only a jest," he stammered. "'Pon my word, Lady Griselda, I meant no disrespect to your esteemed butlers or staff," he said, his face as white as his bald pate.

Griselda's smile broke forth like the sun after a storm, and there was a collective sigh of relief. "Pish-tosh, Albie, it was nothing."

Just then, Christopher announced supper, Bendelson at his side.

Griselda gave a girlish giggle. A nervous, girlish giggle. Her sky blue eyes darted quickly from gentleman to gentleman, and Julie knew her old friend must be in a state of excited agitation wondering which gentleman would find the love charm in his black currant tart.

Oh, la! Julie had to do something. She couldn't let Griselda choose her husband that way! She cursed herself for forgetting about the medallions. How could she have allowed the pleasantness of the day to lull her into such a stupor? She would blame herself forever if she could not find a way to sabotage the medallions and Griselda ended up unhappily wed.

Bendleson stepped aside and held out his hand, indicating that the procession into the dining room should begin, and two gentlemen separated from the crowd, converging upon Griselda. Both were barons and quite equal in status, as their titles had been created on the same day, so neither could claim precedence. They were the highest-ranking gentlemen there and had equal claim to be the one to escort the highest-ranking lady—Lady Griselda, of course—in to supper.

The two stood, red-faced and looking like duelists about to count paces.

Griselda simply laughed, turned, and held out both of her hands. The combatants scurried to be the first to place his arm under hers.

"Come, gentlemen," she said gaily. "My black currant tarts await."

Mrs. Robertson was next with Sir Basil, and then, finally, Julie with Mr. Robertson who, not believing in "all that formal precedence rot" had ducked ahead of where he belonged in the procession, not that Julie minded in the least.

The other gentlemen—one scowling and the rest smirking—fell into step *en masse* behind them.

Mr. Robertson was the answer to her prayers.

A plain-spoken, handsome older man, he had been a servant to Ophelia's family for thirty years before the two had married five years before, to the accompaniment of wagging tongues and lifted eyebrows. Not that either of them cared. Indeed, neither of them seemed to notice, for they'd been too busy noticing each other. Even now, John Robertson watched his wife walking before him and smiled, adoration sparkling in his eyes. He was a good man, sensible and kind, and Julie liked him very much.

The Robertsons were frequent visitors to Alderley

Manor, and, though Julie had spent much time with Ophelia Robertson, she saw precious little of Mr. Robertson, for he was constantly outdoors—not to hunt or to ride, but to lend a hand where he could. He had been a man of all work, but his favorite place was the stable yard, and that is where he could be found most days. He liked to work, he seemed uncomfortable inside, even at mealtimes, and he was even more uncomfortable when company was present.

They were kindred spirits, and they both knew it.

"Black currant, eh?" he whispered as they promenaded into the dining room. "Think your mistress would notice if'n I just pushed it around on my plate some, like we did the rose petals last night? Think she'd notice if I didn't eat none?"

"I—I am not certain," Julie stammered. She hadn't considered the possibility and immediately wondered if there was a way to ensure that Mr. Robertson received the medallion. But his next remark gave her another idea.

"They make me hivey."

"Pardon me?"

"Welts. Black currants make me itch."

"They do?"

"Oh, just so, miss. I shall be sick if'n I eat them. I can't do it. Think she'll notice?"

Julie blinked. "Oh . . . I do not believe it will be a problem."

No, no problem at all. She smiled and patted his hand.

Once in the dining room, Julie excused herself and spoke privately with a footman, who delivered a discreet message to Lady Griselda before the end of the first course: black currants unfortunately

made one of the gentlemen present ill—but Julie
had deliberately neglected to disclose which gentleman it was.

It could not be a fair test if not all of the gentlemen partook, and yet if the others did, the chances
were very good the medallions would be discovered.

Julie knew immediately her gambit had worked.
Griselda's face registered dismay. "It seems the black
currant tarts cannot be served tonight after all," she
announced, "and I am afraid we have no more black
currants with which to make more. I do apologize."

Instantly Julie felt a pang of remorse, for it was obvious Griselda was disappointed.

Stoutly she reminded herself it could not be
helped. If her friend had any chance at wedded
bliss, it could be utterly destroyed by allowing fate to
choose her husband. And while it was true that
every one of the dozen was a good man with whom
Griselda got on well, it was not enough. A husband,
Julie thought, should be a choice of the heart and of
the mind and not of random chance.

Looking away from Griselda, whose eyes had lost
a little of their eager sparkle, she glanced down to
the bottom of the room where Christopher stood.

He was staring at her.

He knew.

The knowledge was there in his eyes, plain to see,
and so was the censure. Their gazes locked and
held. She did not look away. She was not ashamed at
what she'd done. There was no reason to be. She
lifted her chin and eyebrows a notch higher.

Instantly he gave an almost imperceptible nod
and looked away. While he clearly didn't agree with
her actions, he did respect her determination. Julie
felt an inexplicable sense of gratification and relief.

She didn't know why, but she cared what Christopher thought.

"Dewberry!" Griselda interjected from the other end of the table. "Dewberry tarts! Do dewberries give any of you hives?"

She scanned the diners' faces, but no one spoke up. "Excellent!" She smiled beatifically. I happen to know the loveliest little meadow where grow the sweetest little berries—though they do take some hunting to find this late in the season. Who would like to help me?"

Instantly, twelve heads nodded with enthusiasm.

"Splendid!" Griselda cried. "Just splendid. What say you we all go berry-picking on the morrow? We will have nuncheon in the meadow and make an afternoon of it."

There was a cacophony of enthusiastic agreement, and the rest of the meal was spent in endless discussion of the expedition and in endless maneuvering of the dozen for the privilege of driving in Lady Griselda's carriage. Lady Griselda finally settled the matter when she declared Mr. and Mrs. Robertson and Julie would accompany her. It was obvious the dozen did not know whether to feel relieved or disappointed.

The entire discussion should have been vastly entertaining, but somehow Julie could not find it in herself to be amused.

Fourteen

Chris could not find it in himself to be sympathetic.

Despite her assurance to the contrary, Miss Williams had sabotaged Lady Griselda's second go at using the wedding charms, and he'd have wagered his last groat—if he had one—that she had something up her little puffed sleeve this morning, too.

It was past noon, and the day was fine. Rain had given way to a bright, cloud-sprigged sky and a fresh northerly breeze.

Nuncheon was long over, and still the baskets they'd brought along to fill with dewberries were not very full. It was much too late in the season for dewberries, and the tart little fruits were elusive as sapphires.

Chris had come along to shepherd the canine guests, but in truth he'd spent more time keeping the human guests out of trouble. The tall meadow grass waved in the sunshine as the gentlemen roved over the landscape, each trying to outdo the others for the number of berries he could find. So far, Chris had saved one old gentleman from sitting on an ant-infested tree stump, freed another from a bramble patch, where the poor man had become hopelessly stuck, and a third from a mud hole at the bottom of the dell.

When Chris wasn't looking after the canine ladies

or the old gentlemen, he was running to Sir Basil's coach to check on Lady Cowper's puppies—not that they needed checking on, but Sir Basil was more nervous about them than Lady Cowper herself.

He looked over at the coach. Sure enough, there Sir Basil was again, peering into the puppy-crate, which sat in the shade under the coach. Chris smiled and went to stand beside Sir Basil.

"I checked on them not ten minutes ago, sir."

"Eh?" Sir Basil turned. "Oh. Yes, my boy. Quite so. But pups—especially mongrels," he said fondly, "can get into mischief in the blink of an eye, just like any other children."

"Have you children of your own, then?" Chris asked.

"Me?" A curious look entered his eye, half wistful, half amused. "I never married." He tapped the crate with his walking cane. "Not that I did not want to, mind you. A young man ought to marry, if he can. Settles him down." He laughed. "Or so they say." It was clear he didn't reckon himself one of the *settled* group.

"What stopped you from marrying, sir—if I may be so bold?"

"Daft woman would not have me!" He chuckled and then turned to look out across the green meadow. "But old stallions know the road better than the colts, young man, and I realize now it has turned out for the best."

Chris followed his gaze across the sea of waving grass and wildflowers to where Lady Griselda walked with her companion. Sir Basil clucked his tongue. "Deuced capricious lot, women are. You had best watch yourself, young man." He waved his cane toward the two ladies. "Females will rip your heart in

two without trying and never know it." He grunted
and moved off, calling to his dogs, who romped to
his side from every corner of the meadow, their tails
wagging joyfully.

Chris wished he could feel half as much good
spirit. With Edward Cooper in the neighborhood,
Chris was a little worried about what might be going
on back at Alderley—though he'd left the Robertson servants on watch—and even more worried
about what might happen if Edward Cooper and any
possible conspirators decided to pay a call to the
meadow, for there were no servants here but Sully
and Mrs. Mapes. Beyond that, Chris was hot, tired,
covered with mud, and running short on temper.
He fixed his gaze upon Miss Williams. He'd waited
to speak with her all morning. Speak with her, hell!
What he wanted was to shake her, and the chit knew
it. She'd been purposely avoiding him, keeping
close to Lady Griselda so he could not confront her.
Fortunately, Lady Griselda had grown as weary of
her shadow as Chris.

"There," she told Miss Williams. "That looks a
likely spot for dewberries."

"Where?" the younger lady asked, shading her
eyes.

Lady Griselda pointed across the meadow.
"There. Do you see that rock?" A wide, flat gray rock
outcropping lay at the edge of the meadow. "I will
wager there are dewberries hiding there, near that
rock," she said.

"Well then," Miss Williams said with a relieved
glance at Chris, who was clearly edging a little too
near for her liking, "let us go and—"

"I am quite done up," Lady Griselda said, plopping down into the soft grass suddenly.

"I shall stay with you," Miss Williams said.

"No, no, you go on."

"We can look for them together, after you have rested. It would not be right for me to abandon you so."

Lady Griselda laughed. "Surely you jest!" she chortled, glancing about. Seeing that she was stationary, the dozen were converging upon Lady Griselda like happy ants at a picnic. "I need more dewberries." She held out her basket. "Mr. Christopher will accompany you." She waved to him, and he approached.

He gave a low bow. "I shall be pleased to accompany you, Miss Williams," he said. As their eyes met, he allowed his own a malicious glint. "Shall we?" He offered his arm.

There was no escape.

Taking up Lady Griselda's basket, Julie Williams looped her arm through his.

Her bearing was stiff, her hand cool. She'd taken off her gloves to avoid soiling them, and her fingers were stained pink. They walked in silence for a few moments, and then she glanced back.

"There now," she said, "we are far enough away. You may ring a peal over me now."

Chris didn't waste any time. He dropped her arm. "You said you would give the medallions back to her."

"And so I did."

"You deliberately let me believe you would not interfere."

She held his gaze steadily. "I did."

"Yet you sabotaged the black currant tarts."

"Yes."

"And you plan to ruin the dewberry tarts tonight?"

She nodded.

He narrowed his eyes. "How can you do this to her?"

"How can I not?" she answered.

"Are you jealous?"

"Jealous!"

"Is that why you do not want her to marry—because *you* cannot?"

"What are you talking about?"

"Unrequited love," he answered.

"Unreq—I do not know what you are on about."

"You fell in love with someone you cannot have, and so you do not want Lady Griselda to wed, either. She is your friend. You would feel abandoned. Alone. It would bring your own pain more sharply to the surface."

"You do not understand." She turned to walk away.

He grasped her wrist and pulled her around to face him. "Then tell me. Make me understand. Tell me why you would deprive her of marriage."

"Unhand me!"

"Not until you tell me why you would treat Lady Griselda so shabbily."

Indecision marched over her face, only to fall back and give way to a regiment of stubbornness. "Very well. I will tell you—after you unhand me."

Chris let go, and she moved to sit primly on the flat rock.

"Mine was a lonely childhood," she began. "When I was seven, my parents both died of scarlet fever. They left me in the care of an uncle I had never met. Uncle Elbert did not want such a responsibility, but he did enjoy having control of my considerable inheritance—so much so that he planned to keep half of it for himself.

"According to the terms of my father's will, I had to be married in order to inherit," she said, "and even then, of course, my fortune was to go to my husband.

"Since my life was none too happy, Uncle rightly guessed I would marry as soon as possible to escape him. So, at the tender age of fourteen, I was introduced to a friend of Uncle's, Mr. Planck. He was an odious creature, with an overly familiar gleam in his eyes and sweaty palms. He frightened me from the moment I saw him, and even then, I realized my guardian had sold me. The two men, my husband and my uncle, would share my inheritance, which of course would become my husband's immediately upon our marriage. There was no real courtship. Still,"—she shivered—"I was forced to rebuff Mr. Planck's advances, early on. Uncle was furious. He told me I would marry Mr. Planck the day I turned seventeen, or, by God, I would be cast into the street! He locked me out of the house for the night to illustrate his threat. I *was* cold and hungry and frightened—but it did Uncle little good, for I remained defiant.

For the final three years, three years of dread and fear in spite of my own resolve to refuse Mr. Planck, I was tucked away in a boarding school, Baroness Marchman's School for Young ladies. Uncle intended it to be a prison, designed more to keep me from meeting young men than to help me acquire an education."

A satisfied, yet sad, smile ghosted at the corner of her lovely mouth.

"Why do you smile so? What are you thinking?"

She grinned then. "Because . . . Uncle made a grave mistake. The school was run by a remarkably independent woman who had remarkably independent friends—one of whom was Mrs. Ophelia Robertson. I shall give thanks for those gallant and strong women every day of my life!" She closed her eyes and inhaled deeply, shaking her head before she continued.

"One day, I learned to my despair that a wedding announcement had appeared in the newspapers. The date was set for my seventeenth birthday, but I refused to apply for a calling of the banns. Unwisely, I told Uncle that I would wait until I came of age, and then I would marry a man of my own choosing."

"What happened?" he asked softly.

"Within a week, Uncle and Mr. Planck had ruined me, lured me into what looked like a compromising situation and then deliberately exposed me spectacularly, in a very public fashion. I had not yet been presented to the Queen or had any sort of come out, so they did the deed in Hyde Park at four o'clock, in front of God and every wagging tongue in London."

Her face flamed with remembered embarrassment, anger, and humiliation. "No true gentleman would have me after that."

"What did you do?"

"I came away. I bundled up my clothes, sold them in the street, and headed north. I would have roamed the countryside or stayed on the street rather than be forced to marry, but by sheer luck, Ophelia Robertson passed by on the North Road, on her way to Alderley and a visit with her dear friend, Lady Griselda. She saw the fear in my eyes and insisted I come with her. It was by her hand that I was steered to seek a position as Griselda's companion." She sighed tiredly. "I took a false name and disappeared into the country, and I have been happy here ever since."

She looked down at her hands and then back at

him. "You will forgive me if men do not inspire my confidence, Mr. Christopher. It may be, as you said, that it is a man's duty to protect the women in his care, but my experience tells me men often disregard such responsibilities." She looked up at him.

Though her voice was composed and her face impassive, her hands were shaking, her fingers white and knotted together, and he realized how difficult had been her admission.

Suddenly, the heat left her voice, and she looked back across the meadow. "I would stop her from marrying at all if I could, but I cannot. Lady Griselda will wed, but if she is forced to choose, at least she will choose with her heart."

Chris followed her gaze back over the meadow to where Lady Griselda sat. Clustered about her were all but one of the dozen. Off to one side, Sir Basil was still peering under his coach at the pups.

Beside Chris, Julie shifted. "I believe only one of them can make her truly happy," she said.

"Sir Basil?"

She nodded.

"He is a caution," Chris said.

"Indeed."

"An odd duck."

"Yes—and so arse-over-instep in love with Lady Griselda he cannot see straight. Always has been. Watching the two of them with those ridiculous rose petals was almost excruciating." She sighed, stood, and moved toward a clump of bushes and brambles, looking for dewberries. The wind had tugged wisps of her golden brown hair down. They lay crisscrossed over the tender skin at the back of her neck, and he suppressed an urge to brush them away and kiss her there.

He could, if he wanted to.

Sir Basil's voice, calling after the dogs, reached Chris on the wind. Did Sir Basil ever have such thoughts about Lady Griselda? Of course he did, Chris knew. He was a man, after all. A man who'd never married. Had he been in love with Griselda all his long life?

The enormity of it washed over him.

The poor bastard.

What if Julie were right? What if Sir Basil was the one, the right one, the choice of Lady Griselda's heart? What a colossal waste it would be if they did not marry. What a colossal waste it was they had not married years ago!

A wave of desperate empathy rose within him. It may have been driven by his own isolation and sense of loss—he could not say—but he felt the sudden stab of his own loneliness and longing. Mentally thrusting such feelings away, he took a matching step backward.

But the ground crumbled beneath his boot, and then he was falling.

Falling, tumbling. He had a twisting glimpse of the lane far below at the bottom of the rocky cliff, and he knew with a certainty he was going to die. As though from a distance, he heard someone scream—Julie?—and then he slammed to a stop on his back.

A ledge had broken his fall.

Julie's face appeared over the side, her expression wild with fear. "Christopher!" she screamed, her eyes searching. She spied him on the ledge. "My God. Are you all right?"

The fear in her green eyes branded his heart.

It was as though he had been struck by lightning again. Only this time, he hadn't been robbed of his memory but bestowed with sudden understanding, sudden clarity. Time was passing. With each second, a part of his life slipped by, never to be recovered, never to be relived! Each second that passed brought him closer to the last—and one never knew when the last would be. He had cheated death twice, once with the lightning and now with the cliff. It was as though Fate were trying to tell him to pluck the day from the tree of his life and squeeze every last drop of sweet juice from it he could.

He felt reborn.

"Christopher, please! Are you all right?" Julie called down to him once more.

In answer, he grinned and sat up, and then he started to climb.

"Stop that!" she cried. "Stay there. We will lower you a rope."

But Chris did not stop. Never taking his eyes from hers, he climbed the rock face, feeling calm and exhilarated at the same time. She stepped back as he reached the top, but as soon as he gained his feet, he reached out and, pulling her to him, took her into his arms.

"Wh-what are you doing?" she stammered.

"This," he said, and, plucking the sweetest fruit of all, he kissed her.

Her lips were soft, warm. She smelled of lilacs and fear. He nudged her lips with his, bumped them, coaxed them.

"Kiss me," he whispered. "I almost died. I could die tomorrow, today. We both could. Or I could remember who I am and be gone. Kiss me!"

For a second, she stood stiff, uncertain, and then she closed her eyes and melted into his arms. He pulled her to him tighter and pressed deeply. She sighed into his mouth and wound her fingers into his hair.

It was glorious.

It was wrong.

She was married! The thought stabbed Julie and she thrust herself away from him. "I—I am sorry. I was afraid. Afraid you had been hurt. I—I do not know why I. . . ."

"*I* know why. Because you care for me. Because we are meant to be together. I was brought to this place just for that kiss. I was swept here by destiny to show you that time should never be taken for granted. Kiss me again!"

"No! I cannot!" She turned away from him and stilled with shock. Around them stood a ring of raised eyebrows and half smiles. Her cries had brought the entire company running, of course, only to witness the companion kissing the butler like a strumpet at twilight. And they'd heard every word.

"Why not?" Chris asked behind her.

Fifteen

Julie's eyes fluttered open, and she squinted at the afternoon light slanting through her bedchamber window. She'd been lying on her bed since coming home from the meadow. She hadn't bothered to wash or change or even wipe her face. Instead, she'd come home and descended into the troubled sleep of a woman attempting to escape her problems.

Why not? His question was still there, a burr, maddening and sharp. *Why not?*

She'd run from the meadow like a striped ass, leaving him standing there and the question between them. She couldn't answer him truthfully, and after kissing him like that, she couldn't lie, either— though it seemed she'd been doing a good deal of lying to herself.

Since Christopher had come to Alderley Manor, she'd been pretending. Pretending he wasn't really attracted to her, that he wasn't really signaling that attraction, that he hadn't really meant the pretty compliments or the ardent pressing of her hand. And she'd been completely ignoring her own feelings, too, pretending they didn't exist. Oh, yes, she'd acknowledged he was handsome, that she liked to look at him, but she'd been able to push away any deeper feelings—until that kiss.

Since he'd come to Alderley, her feelings had run

the gamut. She'd openly allowed herself revulsion, shock, sympathy, anger, fear, gratitude, guilt, surprise, and pleasure—and she'd acknowledged every one of them, but when he'd taken her in his arms and kissed her, she'd felt more. Much more. With a single kiss, he'd released tenderness, joy . . . and raw desire.

Oh, yes. She'd wanted to go on kissing him. She'd wanted more than that. She'd wanted him to lower her to the grass, to touch her . . . to love her. She'd wanted to *taste the carnal pleasures,* as Griselda had put it.

"A taste—hmmph! La," she told herself, "what you wanted was to have a feast."

She closed her eyes and remembered the strong feel of his arms holding her, pulling her close, the warm scent of him, the softness of his touch. She'd never imagined a man's hard mouth could be so tender. What would it be like if that mouth and those hands were given free rein? A whole night instead of a few seconds, a private bed instead of a meadow surrounded by open-mouthed strangers?

Her body gave an involuntary shiver, and she opened her eyes once more and looked around. The room felt empty.

"Empty," she scoffed. "It is the same as it always has been."

But it wasn't. Nothing ever would be the same.

She'd been so frightened when he'd fallen over that cliff, so afraid of losing him—not that he was hers to lose anyway. He never could be.

She was married.

The room felt empty. The world felt empty. *She* felt empty.

A knock sounded on the door, startling her. She sat

up and wiped at her face, though she knew it would
do little good. She must look a mull. The knock came
again, more urgent this time. It was probably a servant, coming to ask if she wanted supper—or tea, at
least.

"Come," she said, dabbing at her face with the
counterpane as the door opened.

"Think you supper may be a little awkward
tonight?"

She froze. It was Christopher. She heard the door
click softly shut once more, stood, and turned.
There he was, standing in the shadow, like an ap-
parition from one of her uneasy dreams.

The short time at Alderley Manor had worked a
great change in him. Some of the gauntness had left
him, and the wary, suspicious look had disappeared.
He was a startlingly good-looking man—a man who
had taken her into his arms and kissed her but a few
hours before.

"What are you doing here?" she asked, trying to
keep her voice even.

"We need to talk," he said, "and since you will not
come down, I decided to come to you."

She backed away a step. "This . . . meeting here"—
she gestured about them—"is highly improper."

"So was our kiss today in the meadow," he said,
"but that did not stop either of us—at least for a few
seconds."

A denial leapt to her mouth, but she could not
utter it, for it would have been a lie. For those few
seconds in the meadow, she hadn't cared a fig what
was proper and what wasn't—and he knew it.

Reaching behind him, Christopher locked the
door and then took a step nearer. Her heart threatened to pound its way out of her chest. But instead

of pulling her into his arms once more, he sat down next to the fireplace, his eyes never leaving hers.

"We need to talk," he repeated.

"What—what we did in the meadow," she stammered, "the kiss . . . it . . . I—"

He waved her to silence. "We both know all there is to know about what happened in the meadow—not that I intend to ignore it, mind you. In fact, I intend to revisit the subject—though much more thoroughly next time."

She swallowed hard, knowing very well he didn't mean a simple discussion.

His lips curved into a lazy, sensuous smile that confirmed the thought. "But we will need privacy and more time—much more time—for that."

Her heartbeat roared in her ears.

"And, though we have privacy just now,"—he gestured about them—"time is in short supply." His eyes seemed to darken and his gaze slid down to rest indolently on her lips. "Unfortunately." He blinked and gave his head a shake. "There is a more pressing concern," he said. "We must talk about Sir Basil and Lady Griselda."

"What about them?" she asked, though she had a good idea what he would say.

"Sir Basil is miserable. He is, as you said, in love with Lady Griselda. He told me as much today. It is clear to see they are in love, but Lady Griselda is downstairs in the kitchen even now, consulting her household book for a cake recipe. She is stubborn and will persist until your sabotage plans fail and the medallions choose for her."

"I believe she is convinced the medallions will ultimately choose Sir Basil," Julie said.

"I think you are right, and that is why I have come here in secret—to implore you to help me."

"Help you?"

He looked down at his hands and fiddled with his bandage. "Lady Griselda must not be allowed to let the medallions choose. You were right about that, and I was wrong to work against you, but I think you are taking the wrong approach."

"Oh?"

He looked into her eyes. "Instead of stopping the medallions from making a choice, you should help them along. *We* should help them along."

"Help them to choose Sir Basil?"

He nodded.

"It is deceitful," she said.

"Yes."

"Underhanded."

"Yes."

"But not wrong."

"Not wrong," he agreed. "How can it be wrong to bring two people in love together?"

"Perhaps you were brought here to accomplish that."

He stood and moved to within a few inches of her. She could feel the heat of his body, see the tiny flecks of darkest brown in his eyes, yet somehow she found the strength of will to stand her ground.

"I am a messenger," he said at last, tipping her chin up with a gentle touch of his fingertips, "brought here to remind Miss Julie Williams that time . . . is fleeting."

He held her gaze for a few seconds and then dropped his hand and stepped away. "So . . . will you help me?"

* * *

God Almighty, he was either an idiot or a saint.

It had been all he could do not to kiss her. Hell and blast, it had been all he could do not to bed her then and there. She wanted him to. Her pupils had been wide as the Channel, her milky skin flushed pink, her breathing rapid. Oh, yes, he'd had no doubt of her desire. He could have kissed her passionately. He could have carried her to her bed. He could have robbed her of her clothes and her maidenhood and still left her smiling.

He could have kicked himself as soon as they'd passed out of her chamber door.

And now here he was, sitting in the kitchen watching her help Lady Griselda spread a sweet glaze over the miniature pineapple cakes they'd made at one end of the kitchen, while at the far end, Cook and her army of Robertson servants toiled happily away, preparing supper.

According to their hastily concocted plan, Chris had come in a few minutes behind Julie and pretended to be hungry. He ate, while actually keeping his gaze fixed on the pair of cakes that contained the medallions.

He was halfway finished with the strong, sweet tea Julie set before him when he noticed the cup's handle was shaped like an eel. A croaking sound escaped him, and his gaze darted to Julie.

She was staring at him, wearing a knowing, mischievous expression.

He rolled his eyes, and she looked away—before a giggle could escape her, he was sure. He looked down at the eel cup with distaste, but then he smiled. She had a wicked sense of humor he enjoyed.

At last the cakes were covered and set upon a high shelf to cool. Griselda and Julie quit the room to wash and dress for supper, Julie slanting a look from Chris to the cakes that clearly said, *Good luck!*

Taking his time finishing his meal and replacing his dishes on the shelf, Chris waited for an opportunity to mark the medallion laden cakes so they would not be mixed up with the others, but the kitchen was never empty, even for a second. Finally, he simply pulled down the tray and lifted up the cloth cover on the excuse that he wanted to look at them. One, as with all the previous desserts, was marked already with a small mound of sugar. The other had been left unmarked, for Destiny to distribute as she would.

"Still hungry?" Cook asked at his elbow.

Chris turned. "Famished." Behind his back, he gave the unmarked cake a pinch.

"Here then," she said, "I'll just ladle you out a nice cup of that eel soup you like so well." She snatched the eel-handled cup from the shelf and held it up, pride shining in her kindly old brown eyes.

Chris opened his mouth to protest, but what came out was a simple "Thank you," his heart sinking like the heavy chunks of eel in the soup Cook plopped into the cup.

The kitchen didn't have an open window.

Julie could hardly sit still. As the Robertson footman came into the dining room with the enormous tray of pineapple cakes, she realized she was holding her breath.

She'd been uneasy enough before, when all she was doing was trying to stop Griselda from using the medallions. Now, her mind was troubled indeed. For the hundredth time, she asked herself if she were doing the right thing, and Christopher knew. From across the dining room, their eyes met for an instant. He gave a little smile of reassurance and then nodded almost imperceptibly. *Everything will turn out right,* his eyes said.

Julie looked over at Sir Basil, who was staring adoringly at Griselda. At that moment, Griselda, dressed in clear sky-blue satin just matching her eyes, chanced to look up at Sir Basil. He, raising his wine glass, saluted her, and she rewarded him with a soft blush of pink and an even softer smile.

Julie relaxed at last, sure she and Christopher were doing the right thing.

Christopher himself served the little cakes. He'd stayed behind in the kitchen to mark the one with the second medallion in it.

She watched, breathless, as he finally set the last plate down in front of Sir Basil and stepped back, his expression one of deep satisfaction.

No one was allergic to pineapple, none of the cakes had fallen to the floor, and Sir Basil hadn't objected to the color. Everything was perfect.

All of the gentlemen waited for Griselda to pick up her spoon and take the first bite, and then eagerly, they followed suit. As the seconds ticked past and everyone was several bites into the cakes, the tension in the room grew palpable, for Griselda, Ophelia, Christopher, and Julie were all watching, rapt. Watching, waiting for the next bite.

And then it happened.

"What is this?" Sir Matthew Charles said. "I say, Lady Griselda, what a surprise! I did not know you were baking favors into the cake. Am I to be the Lord of

Misrule for the evening? Or have you something else planned?"

Sir Matthew held up one of the shiny gold medallions.

Julie's eyes found Christopher, who stood with his mouth open, shaking his head, his arms having fallen limply to his sides, his face white and stricken.

Ophelia was no better off. She sat biting her lip and looking from Sir Matthew to Griselda, her mouth moving but no sound coming out.

And Griselda? Julie's heart broke when she looked at her old friend, for the blue eyes that always smiled now welled with tears. Covering her mouth with one quivering hand, Griselda shook her head disbelievingly and looked over at Basil. The tears spilled over, and she gave a strangled cry. "No!"

And then the poor dear dropped her spoon and ran from the room, clutching her napkin to her bosom and sobbing.

Ophelia and Julie rose as one and swept from the dining room and into the hall together, an army of two, united in their cause.

"She cannot go where her heart will not," Ophelia said, sailing down the hall.

"We will not allow her," Julie answered, matching Ophelia's swift strides step for step.

Ophelia threw an approving glance at Julie and said, "I admire you, young lady."

"The feeling is mutual," Julie said.

"She went that way!" one of the maids told them at the far end of the hall, pointing toward the front door. It was standing ajar.

Ophelia and Julie hurried outside and saw Griselda fleeing down the hill in the moonlight.

"She is headed for the temple," Ophelia said.

"She often goes there to think. Let us walk and give her a moment to compose herself."

But Griselda wasn't at all composed by the time the other two women arrived. She was crumpled into a sky-blue heap on one of the curving stone benches there, weeping. Ophelia and Julie sat on either side of her and patted her back.

"There, there," Julie crooned.

"Buck up, gel," Ophelia demanded in her own brusque, yet not unkind, way.

"I th-thought—I w-was *certain* B-Basil would be the one!" she sobbed.

"He is," Julie said.

"No!" Griselda cried. "No! The medallions chose Sir Matthew. I am to m-marry Sir Matthew two days h-hence."

"But you love Sir Basil!" Julie said.

"I have made the same argument," Ophelia told Julie over the top of Griselda's hunched-over back. "She will have none of it, the stubborn wench."

Nevertheless, Julie tried again. "Dearest Griselda, the medallions' choice is irrelevant, for your heart has already chosen its mate. You love Sir Basil and he you. You must not resist."

Griselda stilled and sniffled. "You are mistaken. He does not love me."

"Oh, great galloping grandfathers!" Ophelia cried. "Of *course* he loves you, you ninny! Have you heard nothing I have said these past twenty years?"

"Can you not see the longing in his eyes?" Julie asked.

Griselda sniffled some more. "I—I know he cares for me—

"Botheration," Ophelia interrupted her, "why do you think he proposed to you so many times?"

"He was offering for me out of pity," Griselda answered, "but I still thought we were meant to be together. I was certain the medallions would choose him. I thought things would change once we were wed, that he would grow to love me . . . and then just now—the medallion. . . ." Her voice trailed off brokenly, and she waved toward the house.

"Ninny," Ophelia huffed and looked over at Julie. "The message is uncrossed, marked with his seal, franked, and handed to her on a silver salver, but she"—one hand indicated Griselda—"will not read." She heaved a sigh and shook her head.

"Message," Julie murmured. Christopher had said he was a messenger! She smiled and said, "Sir Basil told Christopher he loved you only yesterday."

Griselda stilled and lifted her damp face. First shock and then joy registered upon her features, her smile seeming to light up the entire hillside. "He did?"

Julie nodded.

"Are you quite sure?"

"As sure as Sir Basil loves strays," Julie said.

Beside her, Ophelia cackled.

Julie placed her hand on Griselda's arm. "You can believe it, dearest. Christopher reported the conversation to me himself. Sir Basil said he loves you."

"Sir Basil said he loves me," Griselda murmured. She stood silent for a moment and then hugged herself and twirled around like an excited five-year-old. "He loves me. He *loves* me!"

"Well," Ophelia remarked dryly to Julie, "that settles the matter—thank God."

Griselda and Ophelia spent the next ten minutes waxing rhapsodic about the wedding, chattering happily about the license, the church, the wedding breakfast, the flowers, the guests, and the gown, while Julie sat quietly listening.

She was truly happy for her old friend, but she couldn't help remembering her own long-ago, little-girl wedding dreams and feeling a little sorry for herself.

"Oh! how happy I am Madame Aneault talked me out of the scarlet silk!" Griselda cried and flicked a glance at Julie. Instantly, she stilled.

"Whatever is the matter, my dear?"

Julie shook her head and forced a smile. "Nothing."

"Pish-tosh!" Griselda said. "You look ill."

"She is," Ophelia said. "The gel is love-sick."

"Oh . . . of course she is, and here I am running on and on about my own wedding when our poor girl is sitting here thinking her own day will never come. How insensitive of me!"

"No," Julie said and tried to laugh, but the sound came out more like a sob. "You have it all wrong."

"We do, do we?" Ophelia said.

"I do not love Christopher."

"Do you often go about kissing men you do not love, then?" Ophelia asked slyly.

Julie said nothing.

"Ah-ha!" Griselda crowed. "There, you see? Silence. You are never silent—which means you *do* love him. Shall we make it a double ceremony?"

Julie stood and walked to the edge of the portico. "Marriage is out of the question," she said quietly.

"Do you imagine he does not love you?" Griselda asked. "You did not see his eyes when you fled the meadow after he kissed you, my dear. Trust me, he is a man in love—and I believe you love him, as well. Why is it others can see what lovers cannot? Do you know, you called him Christopher a moment ago. Not

Mr. Christopher, but just plain Christopher—just like you did when he fell over the cliff, only that time you screamed his name. Ah yes, my dear, you are the both of you in love, and I will not end my campaign to see you wed until the church bell is pealing. Why, I—"

"Tell her," Ophelia said, walking to stand next to Julie and poking her with her fan.

"Tell me what?" Griselda asked.

Ophelia bent close. "If you do not tell her, she will not let the matter lie."

"What is it?" Griselda asked, stepping in front of them and looking from one to the other.

Julie sighed and looked down at her hands. "I cannot marry Mr. Christopher, Griselda, for I am already wed to another."

Sixteen

"You are married?" Griselda cried, surprised beyond coherent thought. She didn't know if she'd heard Julie correctly.

Over Julie's shoulder, Ophelia threw Griselda a look of alarm and held one finger surreptitiously to her lips. Clearly, Griselda was to listen to Julie's explanation and say nothing.

Griselda nodded her understanding and sat, and a clearly relieved Ophelia plopped down beside her as Julie began her tale. It wasn't until the very end of the story that Griselda understood the need for Ophelia's warning. Because of it, she was able to keep her face placid when Julie told her she had married a notorious London blackguard.

". . . and then I returned to Alderley," she finished.

"And you never breathed a word of it, my dear."

"There was no need to trouble you," the darling lamb answered.

"And your inheritance?" Griselda asked.

"It is safe, banked in London."

"I gather it is enough for you to set up a household of your own?"

Julie nodded. "More than enough. Much more."

"Then, why—" Griselda began, but Julie held up her hand and interrupted.

"I have no need of it," she said. "I am happy here. I am needed here."

Griselda gave her a wry smile. "You are overworked here."

Julie shrugged. "Where else could I enjoy such a strong sense of purpose? As you now know, I cannot marry and have children of my own."

"Who is this man you married?" Griselda asked.

"There is no use in dwelling upon the matter," Ophelia said quickly, standing up and brushing off her white-gloved hands. "Now the cat is out of the bag, we must let Julie attempt to forget, and mulling the details will not accomplish that."

"Quite right, my dear Ophelia," Griselda said. "We must all of us get on with our lives. Which reminds me—I suspect the supper party is in disarray by this time. Perhaps you should go forth and survey the damage, Julie."

"What shall I tell them? There will be questions."

"Oh, yes, tens of them," Ophelia agreed. "It is no matter. Just smile, say all will be clear on the morrow, and leave the rest to us. Griselda and I will stay here and think of some plausible explanation, will we not?" She nudged Griselda.

"Oh, yes! Yes, indeed," Griselda answered and turned to Julie. "Please do as Ophelia suggests, my dear."

The poor girl trudged away up the hill.

"Why did you not tell me she was married?" Griselda asked Ophelia as soon as her dear companion was out of earshot.

"Because she asked me to keep her secret."

"Confidences can be a bother."

"Indeed they can," Ophelia said. "Now . . . we have

another matter to discuss. What are you going to do about Sir Basil?"

"What about me?" Basil said, appearing suddenly out of the darkness. His black evening clothes had concealed his presence until he'd been almost on top of them.

Ophelia threw a look at Griselda and left without another word.

"What about me?" Basil repeated, sitting next to Griselda.

She did not hesitate but looked him in the eye. "Do you love me?"

His soft brown eyes widened. "I do. I have since the first moment I saw you."

"Why did you not tell me?"

"I did."

Griselda shook her head. "Never," she said. "Never once have you ever spoken those words."

"Bless me, no! I have not. But I *have* told you, my dear, hundreds of times. Thousands. Every speaking glance, every visit, every boring musicale I attended just because I knew you would be there. And then there are the bells, all one hundred and twenty-two of them."

"One hundred and twenty-one," Griselda corrected him.

"I have brought you another," Basil said. "I meant to give it to you if you . . . that is to say, if I. . . ." His voice trailed off. "I hoped to be lucky enough to give this one to you as a wedding present." He took a small box from his pocket and set it upon the stone bench between them.

Opening the box, she discovered a tiny bell of old silver filigree cut-work that curled around the rim and up the diminutive handle, forming dozens of tiny hearts, intertwined and polished and gleaming softly in the moonlight.

"I have a good idea what that favor in Sir Matthew's cake means," Basil said, "and as I am not good with words, I will leave you now. But I hope you will keep this last offering and add it to the others. I beg that you not discard the bells but look upon them in fond remembrance and hear me, each time you hear one of them ring, telling you once more that I love you, for I do love you, Griselda. I always have, and I always will, to the end of my days."

Her eyes misted over, and she threw her arms about him. He responded with surprise and then pulled her into his arms. They'd never embraced, not once in forty years. She was surprised by the strength of him and by the sheer desire she could feel arcing between them. Yet still he was hesitant.

"You have it all wrong," she said, realizing the problem. "My choice is not Sir Matthew. I do not love Sir Matthew. I love you," she whispered fiercely.

He kissed her then, for the first time, deeply, tenderly, lovingly, passionately.

"Does this mean you will keep my bell?" he asked at last, breaking the kiss with an effort that left them both panting.

"I will keep all of the bells, my love. They will stay on the mantel, where they have always been—except for this one, which you must promise to ring for me every night."

"Where will you keep it?" Basil asked, "beside your bed?"

"No," she answered, "tied to the bottom."

Basil kissed her again, and she was lost.

A long time later, when they'd both found their wits and all of their scattered clothes, the image of

Julie's sad face swirled into Griselda's mind, and she sighed.

"What is wrong, my dear?" Sir Basil said, coming up behind her and kissing her neck.

"Julie," Griselda said. "She is in love with your kennel master—"

"Your butler, more like."

Griselda smiled. "How does *our* butler and kennel master sound?"

"Like a proposal," Basil said. "It sounds like a most unconventional proposal."

"I am a most unconventional lady," Griselda said.

"Then you are proposing?"

"Are you accepting?" she returned.

"Indeed, Lady Griselda. I am indeed."

Another lengthy kiss drove all thoughts of poor Julie's plight from Griselda's mind until Basil drew away and asked, "Shall we make it a double wedding then?"

"Nothing would give me more pleasure—well, almost nothing," she said with a playful smile, "but I am afraid it is not to be"—the smile faded from her face—"for it turns out Julie is already wed to another."

"And you want me to leave *now?*" John Robertson asked his wife. "Tonight? Are you daft, woman?"

"It is imperative," Ophelia said. Poor John, he'd only been abed an hour, but it could not be helped. "One of the newspapers must have mentioned him. A viscount cannot simply disappear without anyone taking notice."

"That one could," John said sourly. "He was no good."

"Do not speak of him in the past tense," Ophelia admonished.

"You sure he ain't dead?" John asked. "Mr. Christopher don't look nothin' like that nob, the Viscount Whitemount."

"Nonsense," Ophelia said. "How would you know? He has not been seen in good society for months— and the only time you ever saw him was in the stable once or twice."

"And I never forget a face," John said, "and that ain't his."

Ophelia wandered to the window and looked out upon the moon-bathed night. "He has changed," she murmured. "Both without and within. It is time for him to discover who he is."

"I thought you just said nobody was to know who he is. Isn't that the way Basil and Griselda want it? Didn't you promise Griselda you wouldn't tell no one who he is?"

"*I* will *tell* no one, the newspaper will."

John eyed her meaningfully.

"Yes, yes," Ophelia said, "I know it is stretching the boundaries of honesty, but the situation has changed radically since I made that promise. Miss Williams is in love with him, you see, and everything has changed. She must discover who he is. *He* must discover who he is—or they cannot be together."

"Why not let Griselda and Basil tell him?"

"Because they do not know *who* Julie married, only that she married a dastard."

"I don't understand."

Ophelia walked over to her husband and kissed him soundly. "Of course you do not understand my dear man, for you are a man." She gave him a wicked smile. "There really is no time to lose," she said. I must have those newspapers right away. Go, go!" She pointed to the door. "I promise to explain all later."

"Aye, you old dragon," he said fondly, "but after such a hasty trip to London and all that runnin' about collectin' all those newspapers, I'll expect more than a bit of talk to compensate me when I come back." He gave her a roguish, suggestive smile.

"Aye, you old farmhand," she mocked him, "and after all that explaining *I* shall expect a bit more than what *you* expect." Pulling one of her orange ostrich plumes from her turban, Ophelia wound her arms about his neck and tickled his ear with the feather.

"Promise or threat?" he asked warily.

"Both," she answered with an enigmatic smile.

Seventeen

Two days passed in a frenzy of activity. A license was procured, the church made ready, and even more guests accommodated. Alderley Manor was full to the rafters, and every servant had been working every second. Chris hadn't had even a moment to speak with Julie—not that she'd have been available anyway. She'd been ensconced with the women doing whatever women did before a wedding.

Soon, Chris promised himself, *soon.*

He was standing next to and slightly behind the bridegroom, serving as witness to the marriage of Sir Basil Nairn and Lady Griselda Warring.

Why me? he wondered, not for the first time. Why not Doctor Brown, whom Sir Basil had known for years? Why not John Robertson or even one of the dozen, men who'd run in the same circles as Sir Basil for years. Any of them would have been a more logical choice than Chris. They'd grown old together, after all. They'd seen each other at the opera, at Vauxhall, at balls, and in the park. They'd hunted together, got roaring drunk together, worshipped together, grieved together. They'd vied with each other for ladies' favors and gambled against each other for years. They were friends.

When Griselda's choice was announced, the remaining eleven of the dozen chose to stay for the wedding, and it seemed to Chris all of them had found it in their hearts to be happy for Sir Basil, their rival, and even happier for Griselda, for clearly she was in alt.

So why Chris? It did not make sense, but then he had to concede Sir Basil's choices often made no sense to anyone other than the old man himself.

Chris smiled. Both flighty and unpredictable, kind and happy, Basil and Griselda were a perfect match. They hardly took their eyes from each other the entire service. And when it came time for them to seal the bargain with the ceremonial kiss, both faces shone with an angelic light.

As their lips met, Chris looked over at Julie.

Her expression was tender, kind. She was such a good person.

Compassionate, intelligent, and resourceful, she was slow to pass judgement and quick to help others. He thought of the eel cup she'd given him. It was a kind thing to do—and a mischievous one. She loved such jests, and Chris loved to make her laugh. Everything seemed brighter when she smiled.

A tear of happiness ran down her face, but she was so caught up in empathy with the bride and bridegroom that Chris didn't think she'd noticed.

That was Julie—so concerned for others she didn't pay any attention to her own needs.

Passion, for instance.

She needed passion in her life, yet she kept desire locked away, secret even from herself. But then Chris's kiss had taken her by surprise, and desire had run rampant, if only for a second, before she'd quickly locked it away.

What was she afraid of?

And what would it be like to unlock her desire, to free it permanently?

His senses went a-begging as his mind conjured an image of Julie lying in bed—his bed—her golden brown hair fanned across his pillow, her lithe, warm body waiting naked beneath cold, crisp sheets, waiting for him to—

Permanently?

What lane was his mind travelling?

The marriage lane, came the answer.

He blinked once, twice, and then focused on her shining face and felt his heart beat harder and faster.

Understanding washed over him.

"I love you," he murmured, the words escaping him before he realized it was hardly the appropriate time to make such an announcement.

Too late.

Basil and Griselda broke their lengthy kiss and looked at him, their eyes wide. He had to finish what he'd begun.

"I love you," he said, louder that time. The crowd gasped and stilled. "I love you." It wasn't just about wanting—needing—to kiss her, either. "Marry me," he said.

He could see her pulse beating wildly just above her collarbone. She looked stricken. "I—I cannot!"

He captured her hands in his. "Why not? You love me. I know it."

She shook her head, her eyes wide. "No, I. . . ."

"Deny it, then, if you will."

Tears formed in her eyes. "I cannot," she whispered, her face folding into lines of grief. And, once more, she ran from him. He stood dumbstruck, blinking after her.

"Do not be a lack-wit! Follow her, my boy!" Ophelia Robertson cried.

"But my dear Mrs. Robertson," Sir Basil protested, "you know she cannot marry!"

In answer, Mrs. Robertson only cackled and waved. "Be off, my boy, or you will have the devil of a time catching her! Your sweetheart runs like a deer!"

Chris turned and darted down the church steps.

She'd run down the lane until she'd come to a stile in the stone wall, where she'd turned aside and bolted across a wide field and down a hill, making for the cover of a wood. She did run fast, but she could not match Christopher's stride. He caught up with her just as she gained the first trees.

He dashed in front of her and reaching out, he grasped her arms and brought her to a stop. "Why? Why can you not kiss me? Why can you not tell me you love me? And why can you not marry me?"

Pain shot through her eyes. He could feel it himself, as cold and as sharp as though it were his own. He pulled her into his arms. "What is it?" he asked. "What are you afraid of? Why do you run?"

Her mouth opened, but no sound came out at first, and then she burst into tears. "Oh, Christopher, I do love you. I do!"

He drew her into his embrace. She came willingly, and he kissed her, hard. She responded with heat and intensity that shocked him, drove him to the brink of madness. He lifted her, lowered her into the soft, tall grass at the edge of the wood, kissed her jaw, below her ear, her neck. She arched her head back, moaned, and closed her eyes. Wrapping his arms around her, he pulled her full against him. She rolled across him and kissed him from above, ran her teeth wantonly over his jawline. It was his turn to moan.

She stilled.

"No," she panted, "no. I cannot." She rolled from on top of him and scrambled to stand, clearly shaken.

"If you are worried I am married,"—he shook his head violently and plunged on—"I am not. I cannot be. I likely have no children for one thing, but it is my heart I trust more than that. I know you will not understand—I do not understand it myself—but please believe me when I say my *heart* is certain I have not given it to another."

"No," she said, shaking her head. "You do not understand. It has nothing to do with you. I cannot. . . . we cannot. It can never be."

Bits of grass clung to her gown and her hair. He pulled one long piece away and, placing his hands gently on her sun-warmed shoulders, turned her. "I think it is time you told me the truth. The whole truth."

She met his gaze, her eyes filled with regret. "I cannot fall in love with you, because I am already married."

He fell back, as though she'd struck him a terrible blow.

Julie resisted the urge to close her eyes, to shut out the pain she saw explode onto his face. "I do not love him," she said. "The only time I ever even saw him was on our wedding day."

The story came out in a torrent.

"When I settled here at Alderley, Griselda's independent nature encouraged my own. It blossomed and grew strong. And one day I realized that if my uncle could make a bargain, then so could I." She closed her eyes and told him of her decision to take the journey to Gretna. "Ophelia found my husband for me, a gentleman-who-was-no-gentleman. I had never met him before the ceremony." She told him about her heavy veil and about having taken off her spectacles. "And then, just before I left," she said, "the blackguard stuck his head through my coach's window and stole a necklace that was dear to me, pulled it right from my neck."

She splayed the fingers of one hand against her flesh where the necklace, undoubtedly, would have hung. "I came to believe the impossibility of a real marriage was a small price to pay for a lifetime of freedom and independence."

She opened her eyes and looked into his. "I was wrong. It was a terrible price, for I love you, Christopher. I love you with all my heart."

Taking off his spectacles, he pressed his eyes for a moment and then put them back on. "I care nothing for a marriage certificate. I will have you, take you as my wife, ceremony or no, if you will agree."

"I would, were I the only one to consider, but what if there were children?" She felt the heat climb over her chest and face once more, remembering the passionate embrace they'd shared only moments before.

"Mmmm," he murmured, his mind clearly sifting the same memory as hers. "Oh, yes, there would be children." He sighed and drew her into his arms once more, not a passionate embrace, but a warm, supportive one.

"Come," he said at last. "The wedding party will return to the house soon, and we mustn't allow our sorrow to dampen the day for Basil and Griselda."

With a sad smile between them, they started up the hill toward Alderley Manor.

* * *

The wedding celebration was under way, and the ballroom was full of couples swirling across the floor. Julie and Christopher had returned to Alderley Manor, and they were smiling and apparently carefree, but Ophelia was not fooled. She knew they were miserable.

"Where did you put them?" Ophelia asked her husband, who had returned from London only the hour before the wedding.

"I took them to his bedchamber, as you asked."

Without another word, Ophelia left the ballroom and started for the stairs.

"Here now," John cried, coming along after her, "where are you going, you old dragon?"

"Where do you think, old man? I am going to read those newspapers."

"Not by yourself, you ain't. I'll not have you in another man's bedchamber alone."

Eighteen

"I am sorry for the interruption," Ophelia said, closing the door to the library, where she'd called the meeting. "It cannot be helped."

Inside, Ophelia and Basil, Mr. Christopher, and Ophelia's own dear husband, John, arranged themselves about her, Julie conspicuously absent.

"I say," Sir Basil said, "what is this about?"

"I think I have an idea what it is about," Griselda said, her eyes worried, "and so do you, my dear husband." She threw a speaking glance at Christopher.

"She would not," Basil told his bride. "She promised."

"Oho!" Griselda threw him a look. "You do not know her as I do. She would, if it suits her."

"Mrs. Robertson . . . !" Basil warned.

"I normally do not break promises," Ophelia said, "but I am afraid this time I have no choice." She blew a huge breath up through her magenta feathers, which stuck out from her turban and hung over her face. She hoped to God she was making the right decision.

Taking two newspapers from the table near the double library doors, she handed them to Christopher.

"*The Morning Post*," he read. "The August eleventh edition."

A strangled sound escaped Sir Basil.

"Read it," Ophelia said gently. "The bottom of page six, I believe."

Christopher handed the newspaper back to Ophelia and turned to Sir Basil. "What will I find there?" His eyes were hard.

"Do not be angry," Griselda begged him. "We concealed the truth from you, as you have guessed. But we thought"—she faltered—"we thought it was for the best." She laid a hand upon Chris's arm. "It was a kindness. Truly it was."

"Who am I?" Christopher asked her bluntly.

"I will answer, my dear," Basil said. "It is my responsibility. Keeping it from him was my decision." He exhaled heavily, poured five glasses of brandy, handed them around. Then he took a hefty draught of his own and turned to Christopher.

"You are a man notorious for a very spectacular and very public descent from the pinnacle of society's regard to the depths of debauchery. Your name is George DeMoray."

"George DeMoray," Chris echoed the unfamiliar name in shock.

Basil poured another brandy and handed it to him. "You have not always made the right choices," he said gently, "and I am afraid you have paid for it dearly."

"What do you mean?"

"I was following you at a distance the night you were struck by lightning. You had gambled away the last of your considerable wealth three nights before. You have nothing, my boy. Well . . . almost nothing. You do have one thing." He pulled something from his pocket. "I presume this is yours. I found it in the bottom of my coach. I did not wish to give it to you. I thought it might cause your memories to return." He handed Chris the object, which flashed golden in the August sunlight. "You are a viscount," Basil said.

"A what?" Chris didn't think he'd heard Basil right.

"A viscount," he said again.

Chris felt himself list to one side and sat down heavily. A cold fear had gripped him. It was constricting his chest. He could not breathe. Julie had married a viscount. He looked down at the thing in his hand. It was a gold chain, plain and sturdy but broken near the clasp, and it bore a heavy locket, finely worked with a pastoral scene on the front.

With shaking fingers, he opened the locket to reveal two paintings, miniatures of a man and a woman, Julie's parents. There could be no mistake. The likeness was too close. There were the laughing blue-green eyes, the straight, golden-brown hair, the delicate nose, the generous mouth.

"Why, that is Julie's locket!" Griselda exclaimed, bending close. "She said she lost it on her trip to the Lake District."

"No," Chris said. "I stole it from her—right after I married her in Gretna Green."

Griselda blinked, and understanding dawned on her face as clear as an April sunrise. "Ohhh. Ophelia!" she cried. "You knew about this. Is it true?"

Ophelia nodded. "It is."

Next to Chris, Griselda clasped her hands together. "Oh, Mr. Christopher—dear me, I should address you as my lord, should I not? Oh, you and Julie are wed!" She beamed. "Now you can be together. I shall send for her this instant! How happy she will be!" She reached for the bell rope.

"No!" Chris said. "No. You must not tell her who I am. Not yet. Maybe not ever."

She turned and gave him a quizzical look, a joyous smile still dancing in her eyes. "Why ever not?"

"Do you not see, madam?" Chris said formally. "By all accounts—including hers—I am not worthy of her hand."

"But you have changed," she cried. "It is as though you are an entirely different person—and someday you will be an earl and your financial troubles will be over."

"It is true," Basil agreed. "You are different. Bless me, it is almost as though you have been reborn, my boy."

"He has," Ophelia said. "In a very real sense, he is no longer George DeMoray. If he chose to remain Mr. Christopher, he could."

Griselda scoffed. "Why would he do such a thing? Then he could never marry Julie."

"He could if he waited seven years," Ophelia said. "He could marry her as Mr. Christopher Christopher."

Chris nodded. "Or she could be free to marry someone else, someone worthy of her."

"Worthy of her!" Griselda cried. "You *are* worthy!"

"Am I?" Chris asked.

London was a swirl of noise and fog and mud. It had rained all the way there. Shivering in spite of his borrowed greatcoat, Chris—for so he still thought of himself, since his memory hadn't returned—dismounted in front of a tall, narrow townhouse in Silver Street with the numeral 7 over the door. It was, apparently, the house he'd gambled away over a fortnight ago, when he'd lost his last farthing.

He'd come to answer his own question. Was he worthy of Julie? "Who am I?" he murmured. Who was this George DeMoray—the man who gambled away a fortune, the man no one cared for enough to find, the viscount whose disappearance almost no one had noticed?

Tying his horse, he climbed the steps and knocked upon the door. A fetching young woman answered, a maid, by the look and sound of her.

"Yes?" she asked, looking Chris up and down and clearly finding him lacking. "What do you want?" In spite of the dark wig he wore and the fine set of clothes Doctor Brown had lent him, she didn't recognize him. His friends in Alderley had tried to warn him no one would recognize him. Even so, they'd advised him to purchase the wig, dress more as he used to, and remove his spectacles before showing himself.

"Good day," he said, taking off his spectacles. "My name is George DeMoray, and I—"

She squinted at him, gasped and, looking over her shoulder, came onto the steps and quickly closed the door after her. "I'm sorry, my lord. I didn't recognize you at first. You look different. What's happened to you? Crikey," she rushed on, not waiting for an answer, "you shouldn't be here." She looked nervously around. "If they was to find you. . . ."

"Who?"

"Them what's lookin' for you—beggin' your pardon. The ones you owe. They been 'ere day and night to dun you, sir. Ringin' the bell at all hours. The new master would like nothin' better than for them to find you, my lord!" She looked furtively about them a second time before looking back at Chris. "Did—did you come here for me, my lord?" She looked hopeful and yet wary.

"No," Chris shook his head. "I did not know you would be here." It was true enough.

The maid licked her lips, her expression wary. "See here, I'll take half what you used to give me, seeing as how you've hit a spot of rough in the road." Fear made her eyes cloudy as she rushed on, "I'd do it with you for free, I'm that glad to see you, but me mum, she's taken a bad turn, and there's hardly a crumb in the—"

"What is wrong with your mother?"

"Why, 'tis her heart, my lord. Same as always."

Without hesitating, Chris reached into his pocket. The poor maid flinched, and Chris realized she'd expected him to strike her when she saw his arm move. He felt ill.

He took out one of the guineas he'd borrowed from Doctor Brown before leaving Alderley. Placing it in the maid's palm, he curled her fingers over it. Her eyes grew round.

"I am not going to hurt you," he said. "I do not want to—to lie with you."

"What *do* you want, my lord?" Clearly, she didn't believe him.

"I want you to talk to me. I need some information."

"Talk," she said flatly.

"Yes. I need you to tell me about myself."

When Chris had explained he'd lost his memory and convinced the maid she could keep the golden guinea for doing nothing more than talking, she was happy enough to oblige. Chris flagged down a hackney coach and spent a half-hour hearing all the girl knew about George DeMoray.

It was worse than he'd imagined.

As Basil had said, George DeMoray, the Viscount

Whitemount, had been at the pinnacle of society's regard. But he'd arrived there through a series of strategic liaisons and betrayals.

Apparently, he'd crowed over his successes to the pretty maid as he'd used her, knowing she would not dare speak of it to anyone, for although she was afraid of him, she needed the money he occasionally gave her. It could not have been enough.

As he rode away, he shuddered.

Making his way through Mayfair, he stopped at a house the maid had directed him to, this one far grander than his own—and it had the advantage of not having been lost at the faro table by its owner, who happened to be George's father, the Earl of Westfold, if the maid could be believed.

George had begun to doubt the veracity of her story. He was forced to wonder if she wasn't making up some or most of it. He just couldn't imagine himself doing all of the terrible things she'd mentioned.

Neither could he imagine any father failing to notice his own son's disappearance or not being overjoyed at his return, but as soon as the door of his father's house was opened and he told the butler his name, the door was shut without another word. Apparently, the earl's son was a pariah, unwelcome at any time and for any reason. Chris stood on the doorstep blinking in shock, an empty sadness infusing his existence. Yesterday morning, he'd longed for a father, never imagining that having one could be worse than having none.

His next stop was his stepmother's townhouse. According to the maid, she and the earl had lived apart for many years, ever since Chris was a lad, and their enmity was a well-known item of gossip and source of amusement among the *ton.*

Chris was glad to be shown in as soon as he announced himself—though his sense of relief was short-lived.

After waiting for almost an hour, the butler returned. "Her ladyship will see you."

A footman bade Chris follow and led him to a second floor hall with doors opening on either side. The servant stepped aside, clearly expecting Chris to know which door to choose.

"I . . . am afraid I do not remember the way," Chris said.

An incredulous look escaped the man's face before he mastered it and said, "Yes, my lord. Of course, my lord," and he led Chris down the hall to a door, bowed, and then swiftly retreated as though wary of whatever was behind the door.

Chris watched him disappear down the hall and then put his hand on the knob. "It does not look like the gate to hell," he said wryly.

He was wrong.

As soon as he opened the door, he saw her. She was younger than he expected her to be. Dressed in a transparent wrapper, she sat on the wide windowsill, deliberately allowing the sunshine to render her silhouette visible, her blonde hair unbound and curling about her shoulders. She was beautiful.

As he stepped forward, she slid her rounded bottom onto the edge of the windowsill and, bracing her palms on the edge, spread her heels apart. There was no mistaking the gesture.

"You could not stay away," she said. It was a statement, not a question.

Was this his stepmother? She could be someone else, he reasoned, a housekeeper perhaps or a guest of the Countess's, a lady he was supposed to know. "Lady Westfold?"

"Oh-ho! My, George, how formal we are!" she laughed, a sound devoid of any merriment, and instantly Chris's mind compared it to Julie's genuine laughter. Whereas it always made him feel happy inside, the Countess of Westfold's laugh made him feel . . . forlorn.

"I wish to speak with you," he said.

"Talk," she said, "how novel." She flowed off the sill, a river of perfumed, silken femininity, and, wrapping herself around him, kissed him briefly, her tongue teasing suggestively. Then she moved to the bed and, opening her wrapper and herself to him, displayed herself across the pink satin surface. "Enough talk," she said. "Come to me." It was an order. "You have neglected me these six months. I may have forgotten where my pin money is kept. If you jar me hard enough—uncommon hard— perhaps I will remember."

It was then Chris noticed the bed hangings.

They were pink lace.

He staggered and clutched at the bedpost as the image broke the dam of his memory, and his past flowed into his head like a torrent. All of it—his childhood, his parents, his rise to the pinnacle of society, his cruelty and his betrayals, his ignoble downfall, his marriage to Julie.

"Come," his stepmother commanded.

Bile rose to his throat, and he shook his head. "I am sorry, Lady Westfold, but I will no longer . . . jar you. I came to talk, but now there is no need."

With his memory intact, there was no longer any need to gather information from others.

Her brown eyes turned to stone, cold and unyielding, and she sat up, making no attempt to cover herself, her breasts jutting between the folds of her untied wrapper. "Do not attempt to extract more from me than you are used to receiving. It is a well-known fact you are in even worse straits than you were six months ago." She smiled. "Oh, yes, I heard the news. You have lost everything. You are in worse need of my pin money than you were before. You have thinned, by God, and I will wager you would take half what I used to give you, just to feed yourself." With these words, she could not hide a sneer. "But I suppose all of my pin money could not end your current difficulties. You are in too deep. Perhaps now you will consider my offer."

She stood and walked into her dressing room.

"Which offer is that?" Chris said. She had made him so many over the years, and they were surfacing in his memory from the depths of his past like bubbles rising through dark, thick water.

She gave an unladylike snort. "You know deuced devilish well what I want." She smiled, a lazy expression he could see did not reach her eyes. "My offer stands," she said. "I will pay your debts with my own fortune in exchange for half of the transferable assets you inherit when Westfold gifts us with his departure from this world—may he roast in hell." She emerged from the dressing room wearing a lavish teal gown and carrying a paper, which she tossed down onto the bed. "I would put it on the dressing table in deference to your change of heart, darling, but old habits are hard to break, and we have always conducted our most important business right here. Sign it."

"And if I do not?"

She gave a brittle laugh. "I have nothing to

threaten you with anymore, not after you told the earl about us yourself. But it is no matter. If you do not sign today, you will soon. You do not wear poverty well, darling."

A bell sounded somewhere in the house below them, and her eyes darted to the door. "Ah, my other guests have arrived, no doubt."

"What other guests?"

"No one you know," she said. "Come. If you will not sign the paper, then I will escort you to the front door."

"No need," he said. "I know the way."

"Ah, but I insist," she said, her voice sibilant and low. She moved quickly to the door. Chris followed her down the stairs and to the front door, where stood the butler. "Where are my friends?" she demanded.

"Waiting outside, my lady," the butler answered.

Waiting outside? Chris felt a thrill of alarm as the countess swept to the door.

"Sign the paper now, Whitemount," she said, "or my friends will escort you to a place where making the decision to sign will be much easier." She pulled the door open and stepped aside, revealing three rough-looking men on the step. "Debtors' prison is not a pleasant place, I'm told. Do reconsider, darling."

At a nod from the countess, the three men surged through the opening, lunging toward Chris. Sparks careened through his veins and he jumped back, spun away, and fled through the house.

Nineteen

Delivered from London to an inn at Buxley-on-Isis:

> *Arriving late tonight. Wait on the road at the top of Alderley Hill.*

Bounding down the hall, he ran for the back door, his pursuers' footfalls percussing off the walls like huge drums of warning, spurring him on until he reached an outside door and flung it open.

When he'd been shown inside, he'd handed his horse—borrowed from Doctor Brown, like everything else he had—over to a groom. The animal would have been taken to the stable yard, he knew. Looking wildly across the grounds behind the house, he spotted the stable barn and dashed for it, the three men right behind. Darting inside, he spotted the horse right away. It was still saddled and bridled, standing at the other end of the barn, next to the far door. The poor beast's eyes rolled white as Chris ran toward it, the three men in pursuit, but it could not be helped. Still not entirely recovered, he'd have no hope of escape without the horse. He could not depend upon his own legs to outrun his pursuers.

Behind him, he heard the stable door clang shut

and a shadow fell over the hard-packed, sawdust-covered floor. The three had come into the stable and shut the door behind them, blocking that way of escape, but it was no matter, for there was a far door. They'd lost precious seconds in closing the door behind them. It was a miscalculation. All Chris had to do was mount and kick the bar on the far door open, and he would be free. But just as he rushed headlong toward his horse, a fourth man stepped from the last stall, barring his way. The horse reared and screamed. The man laughed.

There was no escape.

Chris skidded to a stop and stood there, panting, as the men closed in upon him from both sides. He should have known there would be trouble when he'd not seen any stable hands about. Backing against one wall, he braced himself against his knees and eyed the men. "Four against one," he drawled. "Not very sporting, is it?"

"We ain't lookin' for sport, gov, it's the money we're after. A hefty reward's offered for you. Come easy-like, and I promise we'll treat you gentle." The man took a step closer to Chris, flexing his large hands. He didn't look the gentle sort.

Good God, what was going to happen to him when they caught him? He'd be thrown into the King's Bench or Marshalsea prison and sit there until he rotted—or until he signed that paper of Lady Westfold's. He knew Ophelia or Basil and Griselda would come for him if they found out, but they would never hear of it unless it were from his own lips. No one would know he was there until he left the place. He had no doubt the countess would pay the gaoler to forget he was there, because that's what Chris-as-George would have done—*had* done—given a similar situation. A vi-

sion of Julie blew into his mind like a summer breeze
turned cold.

She, along with everyone else at Alderley, would
think he had abandoned her.

In desperation, Chris dashed into one of the stalls
and slammed the door shut. Looking around for a
way to secure it, he seized on a pitchfork and wedged
it tightly, tines down, between the earthen floor and
the door bracers with a hard stomp of his foot.

Outside, the man laughed harder. "Look 'ere lads,
the dicked-in-the-nob nob has locked himself in!"

Chris looked around him. There were no other
windows or doors, and the rafters were high out of
reach. Two stalls away, a ladder stood in the corner—
but the stall in between was a disconcertingly small
space occupied by a disconcertingly large and very ag-
itated stallion bent upon kicking the walls down. That
way led to almost certain injury and possible death.
And yet, a moment later, Chris had vaulted atop of the
half-wall separating the stalls.

He'd cheated death before.

The four men, who had been laughing and peering
into the stall stopped laughing and watched in amaze-
ment. The stallion reared, stabbing the air with
hooves and shrieks of rage, and when it touched
down, Chris leapt onto the beast's back and then with
another great leap jumped into the far stall.

The men realized what he intended then, but it
was too late, for by the time they'd made it into the
stall, Chris had already scrambled up the ladder and
thrown it down into the stallion's box. He didn't
wait to see what they'd do next. Running atop the
rafters, Chris sprinted for the end of the barn,
pulling his cravat from his neck as he went and wrapping it around one hand. At the end of the barn, he

grasped both sides of the rope used to raise hay, one side in each hand, and lowered himself to the ground in seconds, kicking the outside latch closed as he passed.

The door complained as the men unbarred their side and attempted to open it. They swore and crashed against it once, twice.

"Stop that, you clods, he's runnin'!" one shouted. "Out the other end! Be quick!"

But instead of running, Chris hovered next to the door as the men's heavy footfalls retreated, and then he heard shouts as they emerged from the other end and split into two groups of two and came down either side to trap him. Waiting almost until they rounded the end of the barn, Chris unlatched the door and slipped back inside. It was empty, and there was his horse. Vaulting into the saddle, he kicked the horse into a run and streaked through the open door at the far end.

As he passed by the back door of the house, he caught a glimpse of the countess standing there in the open doorway. She'd seen everything, knew he had escaped her, and though he would have expected her to wear a disappointed, angry expression, the only thing he could see on her face as he passed in those few seconds was surprise, surprise and lust. She obviously hadn't expected George DeMoray to try escaping, especially in such a manner—no one who used to know him would have—and the knowledge made her want him even more.

As he urged his horse northward through the maze of streets, Chris only felt pity for her—something else none would have expected from George DeMoray, he knew. But there it was. He did feel sorry for her. A mile went by, and he slowed his horse to a walk.

Locked into a loveless marriage, his stepmother was a prisoner of her own making. She could have escaped the life she led if she'd abandoned her pride. Her personal fortune was more than enough to support her, if she would but set aside her title and disappear into another existence as Julie had.

Or as he could.

He gave a pat to his tired horse. The houses had thinned, and he was on a little-used road he knew. Further on, it dwindled until it was hardly more than a footpath before it merged with the Great North Road. There had been no sign of pursuit, and he knew he was safe. He sighed and, coming upon a water trough, dismounted to give his unfortunate beast a rest.

"By Jove," he said aloud, "I could do *exactly* as Julie did." He could return to Alderley and discard his old life entirely. He would never have to tell anyone who he really was. Basil and Griselda and the Robertsons would keep his secret, he was certain. He'd have no title, no fortune to inherit, but he would have a new life, a new beginning. And when George DeMoray had been missing long enough to be declared dead, he would have Julie.

"Christopher Christopher," he murmured. That is who he would be for the rest of his life. He would escape his old persona, his old existence. He *deserved* to escape it, for he wasn't the man he once was. George DeMoray had reveled in the terrible things he'd done, celebrated them. But Chris Christopher was appalled at them, and he could never escape the shame of what he'd done—especially what he'd done to Julie.

He'd done more than take half her fortune and steal her locket. She didn't even know about what he'd done, and he could never tell her the truth, for she would never forgive him.

And he wouldn't blame her.

George DeMoray was a scoundrel, a dastard, a blackguard. In his quest to reach the peak of society's regard, he'd betrayed confidences, lied, cheated at the card table, ruined others willingly. He was intelligent and cunning, and he was good at being bad, his victims never even suspecting what he'd done, which had given George much pleasure. Oh, yes, he'd enjoyed great success—until he'd targeted the wrong person, The Gypsy, Artemis Rose. It had been a grave miscalculation. She'd been a favorite of the prince and been fast becoming a darling of the *ton,* and to make things worse, she'd belonged to his fiercest rival. George DeMoray had tried to ruin her and ruined himself instead.

Thrown down from the peak of his success by none other than the prince, he was snubbed *en masse* by every London host and hostess who'd been too afraid to snub him before. His creditors rushed to collect, rightly suspecting that none of them would be paid. George simply hadn't the blunt. He'd been living upon the expectation of his inheritance, borrowing against the fortune everyone knew he was to inherit upon his father's death. He'd been dunned unmercifully. People he'd cut weeks or months before took pleasure in giving him the cut now. He was refused admittance to Almack's and, finally, to his clubs.

He'd retreated into his house, angry—and frightened, though he hadn't admitted that to himself, at first, and he'd taken out his despair and confusion on his staff until they all left him—all but the little maid, who needed the pittance he sometimes tossed her too much to risk leaving.

Sometimes she'd cried as he mounted her.

The memory was too much for him. Sinking to the ground, his back to the stone trough, he bowed his head and wept for a long time, not out of self-pity but out of remorse for all the horrible things he'd done.

Next to him, the horse whickered and nudged his head and then wandered over to the side of the lane, cropping the tufts of lush summer grass there, and Chris sobbed, wracked with pain and regret.

A long while later, when his eyes were hot and dry and he could cry no more, Chris looked up. The horse's flanks had dried, and the animal was standing on three legs, peacefully asleep. Chris was glad the beast had suffered no lasting ill from the morning's misadventure. That was the only similarity between himself and George DeMoray, kindness to animals. Though George had never gone out of his way to be kind to a person, animals were another matter. When he was a little boy, sometimes his parents' visitors brought along their own dogs, and he'd enjoyed cavorting with them much more than he'd enjoyed being with people. Dogs enjoyed being with him, went places with him, loved him. But they always left.

As an adult, George had always wanted a dog or two, but he'd been away from home so much he knew they'd come to love the servants more than they would him, so he never had any."

No wonder he'd taken so to Sir Basil's pack!

The clouds had dissipated and the sun was getting higher and hotter. Chris's head itched. Reaching up, he grasped the dark wig he'd purchased in London, pulled it off, and threw it into a field. Now he knew why they'd been so adamant he procure the thing and dress like the Town buck he'd been before. They'd known he wouldn't want anyone to know what he really looked like these days.

George took off his coat and tucked it into a saddlebag. It was going to take him months to earn enough to pay the doctor back for his ruined cravat, abandoned greatcoat—which was still at the countess'—and the money he'd borrowed. But Chris couldn't think of anything else he'd rather be doing than living and working at Alderley Manor. He was needed there. No one had ever needed him before. His help was appreciated there, even when it caused more problems than it solved, and that felt good.

Chris mounted and started back down the track, feeling better than he could ever remember feeling, in spite of the guilt he carried. George DeMoray had never experienced guilt before, and so even though it was a terrible burden, Chris was proud to carry it.

For the first time in his life, he was returning home to a place that actually felt like home, a place where he was needed and wanted, the place he belonged. And the cornerstone of it all was Julie—his wife, though he would not tell her that. No, he would court her devotedly until George DeMoray was declared dead, and then Chris would marry her, this time in a church, with flowers and a proper wedding gown and anything else she thought she might need. She deserved no less.

"Ah . . . and a proper wedding night—if I can wait that long."

He would wait, too. They would marry again and have children—legitimate children. Children who would carry the name of Christopher.

"I am Christopher Christopher," he said and laughed, feeling quite carefree now. It felt so good to have escaped, to be free, to be reborn.

It was the happiest day of his life, so far, and the further north and west he traveled, the better he felt. He stopped at a small inn early in the evening with the intent of staying overnight, but after having his meal, he decided to push on. He was no more than six hours from Alderley, and the doctor's horse was used to traveling long distances and at all hours. Buying a lantern from the innkeeper at an outrageous price, Chris set out once more.

His heart swelled with gladness as he finally climbed the last dark hill and saw the windows of Alderley Manor softly aglow. Safely on the lane, he put out the lamp, the better to enjoy the sight. A sense of peace enfolded his heart, and he smiled. Julie was in there.

But his sense of peace was short-lived, for as he approached the house, he discovered his new life tumbling down upon them all.

Twenty

The first thing he noticed was that the watch was gone. There was no sign of the two men who were supposed to be on guard. Two horses stamped and fretted outside as though they'd just arrived. No one had attended them, and they were tied to the front portico's columns to await their riders. With shock, he recognized one as Edward Cooper's mount. Edging closer, he looked around and listened.

The library was ablaze with light. The day had been hot, and the windows there were still open. An unfamiliar male voice carried outside, calm and even, but something in it sent a chill down Chris's back.

"He is dead."

Vaulting from the saddle, Chris ran silently to the window, hunched so as to escape detection. He didn't know what he'd see, and his heart felt like thunder in his chest. He peered inside.

At one side of the library stood Julie, with Basil and Griselda flanking her. Julie's expression was full of defiance as she stared coldly at two men standing opposite her, but Chris watched Griselda and Basil trade looks full of fear. Chris knew why, for he recognized one of the men as Julie's uncle. The other was Edward Cooper, the stranger he'd met on the road—though Chris realized with a sudden shock that Mr. Cooper was no stranger, after all. Chris had known him for a long time, though the man had used a different name—Howard Planck, the one her uncle tried to force her to marry.

Instantly, Chris's blood was on fire, and his palms itched with the desire to expel the two from Alderley Manor.

They were both big men, not quite as tall as Chris, but certainly heavier. He would need the element of surprise to bring them down if needed, and so he decided to remain silent and ready to spring through the window.

"When did this happen?" Basil asked.

"On the fifth," the younger man said, "which is ironic, for that is how much whiskey he consumed that night."

Basil and Griselda glanced at each other again and then back at the men, fear evaporating from their hardening expressions, their bearing stiffening into fierceness. Silence descended upon the room, and Chris could hear the mantel clock ticking.

Julie's eyes never left the older man's. "What do you want of me, Uncle?" she asked at last.

"Do you not wish to know how he died?" her uncle said and then smiled. "How very callous, my girl."

"I am not yours, and I never was," Julie said tightly.

Elbert Fitz ignored the remark. "We were on a packet ship heading north out of Newcastle-upon-Tyne and ran into bad weather. Whitemount was swept over the side and lost."

Whitemount! Chris felt him himself blench.

"Saw him go under myself," Elbert said. "Several of the crew saw it, too. They'll swear to it. His body was never recovered."

"What do you want?" Julie asked again, her voice amazingly steady.

"What do I want? Only that which is my due. I feel I'm owed something for taking you on. Ain't easy for a bachelor to take care of a brat. Ties him down."

"You exaggerate," Julie said. "I was no bother to you. You sent me off to Wessex, and I barely saw you—you or anyone else—until my fourteenth summer."

"You were better off there. I knew nothing about caring for a little girl. When you were old enough to carry on a conversation and do more than play with dolls, I brought you back to London."

"You put me in a boarding school."

"Yes, and it was not cheap."

"Ah!" Julie said, eyeing him knowingly. "Money. That is what this visit is about, is it not? Let me guess, you want me to sign over my fortune to Mr. Planck, here?"

The uncle did not attempt to deny it. "Now your husband is dead, I am hoping you will do the right thing and give Mr. Planck his due. Your fortune should have been his. He was counting on it, and he has debts because of it. The money is rightfully his—what's left of it, after you gave half to Whitemount to squander." He curled his lip in distaste.

"Ah. Yes," Julie said sarcastically, "let me just sign over my entire fortune to a stranger. Does anyone have a quill at hand?"

"See here, my girl," Elbert said, taking a step closer, "it was you who cried off the engagement, leaving Howard high and dry."

"Howard, is it? How curious a lady should not know her former fiancé's given name," she remarked with studied boredom and picked at a nonexistent flaw in the blue damask of the sofa.

Elbert's color was rising, and his voice took on a shrill quality. "If you think you can—"

"I never agreed to the engagement," Julie interrupted, looking him square in the eye. "In fact, I made it clear to you and to the ladies who ran the boarding school—one a baroness of unimpeachable reputation and another who has since become the Viscountess Trowbridge—that I would not have him." She tilted her head toward Howard Planck. "And I did so long before you placed the announcement in the newspapers. There are many who know you did not have my assent, and no ring was ever exchanged for the simple reason you knew I would toss it into the Thames the first chance I had."

"Mrs. Drummond-Burrell saw you participating in a tryst with a ring on."

She glowered. "Mrs. Drummond-Burrell saw me being attacked and throwing a ring to the ground— a ring that was forced onto my hand only seconds before."

Her uncle smirked. "Perhaps, but no one believed you, did they? No, they all thought you were a wanton filly who did not wish to wait for your wedding, one who balked when she was caught."

Julie blinked and her mouth twitched before she said, "That is correct, Uncle. And since my reputation is in tatters, and there is nothing I can ever do about it, it cannot hurt to be found not *doing the right thing,* as you say. So, if that is all you have come for, Uncle, I will ask you to leave now, for we are tired and need our rest."

Elbert exchanged a smug look with Howard Planck, pulled a paper from his pocket, and threw it down onto the round library table. Julie's eyes flicked toward it, but she remained motionless. Inside, Chris cheered.

"The sailors are also ready to swear you were aboard that ship with us," he said.

"Outrageous!" Basil cried. "She was right here at Alderley Manor, and we can prove it."

A smile slid onto Elbert Fitz's face. "I think not."

"Balderdash!" Basil snarled. "I will not stand for any more of this. Get out before I throw you out."

But the men ignored him, and Howard Planck turned to Julie with a sneer. "Tell them," he ordered.

Julie exhaled and dropped her eyes, and Chris was dismayed to see defeat shaping her figure. "I was in Northumberland on the fifth of August," she said.

"In the company of two menservants," Griselda protested. "They will swear you were not aboard that ship."

But Julie was shaking her head. "When we arrived in Northumberland, Sully and Wells were tired, and I was worried about them. Over their protests, I went about on my own for three days and did not find—"

"Oh, my!" Griselda cried. "You went about on your own? With no chaperone? That is not done, my dear. It is not the thing!"

"I *am* a servant, my lady," Julie said formally, "and a married servant at that, one well past the first blush." As she reassured Griselda, Chris was amazed and humbled to see the barest hint of a fond smile crook the corner of her mouth. Even in the most desperate circumstances, Julie's good nature did not desert her. "As I was saying," she continued, "I did not find the red house until our journey home."

"Perhaps because you had no intention of looking for it at all, at first?" her uncle said, smiling openly now. "I am afraid she had another purpose in Northumberland than to find your ridiculous red house, Lady Griselda."

"Red house?" Basil asked.

Griselda shushed him. "I will tell you about it later, my darling."

"Your companion had no intention of returning with the menservants," Elbert Fitz said. "She was going to leave your service and come away with Whitemount, whom she had arranged to meet."

Julie looked at Griselda and shook her head emphatically.

"Do not worry, dearest," the old lady replied. "I would not believe this man if he said it was daytime while the sun shone."

Elbert Fitz gave a greasy laugh. "Whitemount was making for Scotland, where he had hidden some of his assets. But he hadn't told his wife where, and when he was swept overboard, your *dearest* was so overcome with fear at being alone in the world, she married Mr. Planck here, right away. Then she had a change of heart and left her poor husband—just like she left when they were engaged, just like she did Whitemount after she married him—and she fled back here to Alderley under her assumed name, thinking to get away with it just like she had the first two times."

"No one will believe you," Basil said.

"We've a Scots parson and witnesses who are ready to swear to the marriage," Fitz said, "and I have the marriage certificate right here in my pocket."

"It does not bear my signature," Julie cried.

"Oh yes. Yes, it does," her uncle said. "You see, I can sign your name better than you can, my girl. I have had years to perfect the skill. And, since there's no denying you married and then ran away once before—to say nothing of running away from an engagement—I doubt very much a court would find your denials credible, especially with your own guardian speaking against you."

"You scapegrace!" Basil cried. "The marriage is a fabrication. No one will believe such a Banbury tale." He advanced a step and shook his fist.

Julie touched the old man's shoulder. "It is no use, sir. What he says is true. I would not be believed."

Elbert Fitz tapped the paper on the table and turned back to Julie. "This document gives control of your remaining fortune over to Mr. Planck. Sign it and we will disappear into the night, and your marriage to Mr. Planck will never have happened. Sign it, or by God you shall come away with us this night and never see this place again!"

Julie looked down at her hands and then walked to a writing desk and retrieved a quill.

Griselda gave a cry of dismay. "You will not sign it, will you?"

Julie shrugged. "It would seem I have no choice."

"Do not touch that quill." Basil advanced upon the two men. "I will take care of this!" His eyes were grim and angry, and Chris had no doubt Basil meant it. The old boy was going to attempt to thrash them. Chris put his hands on the windowsill and tensed to spring through, but Julie intervened.

"No, Sir Basil!" She put her hands upon his arm and tugged him to a stop. "I do not care about the money. What do I need it for? I have not touched a farthing of it since I gained control of it. Griselda pays me well, and I have all I need or want here. If I give the money to these men, they will go away, and I will never have to think of them again. I shall be happy once more."

"But what if Whitemount is not even dead?" Basil said. "What if they made that up, too? The newspapers say he is missing, but what if he shows up? He will refute their story."

"We thought of that," Howard Planck said and smiled. "If Whitemount shows up, then my lovely bride here could be accused of bigamy, an offence punishable by seven years' transportation."

"She is caught," Griselda whispered, the horrified sound carrying easily over the silence that had descended.

Julie picked up a quill. "I will sign."

Outside, in the darkness, it was as though time had stopped. Chris's heart felt as though it would never beat again.

He knew he had a choice.

He could walk inside, or he could walk away.

It was clear Basil and Griselda had kept the secret of his identity from Julie as he'd asked them to. Julie didn't know Chris was George DeMoray—but her uncle and Mr. Planck would, were Chris to appear inside, for he'd helped them ruin her.

He'd played a minor role, really, but it had been a pivotal one. He'd been riding by on that day in Hyde Park, when Elbert Fitz had called out to him. Would George care for a little sport? he'd asked with a malicious glint in his eye. George had found such an offer irresistible, and on a lark, he'd helped Fitz, leading Mrs. Drummond-Burrell over to a secluded little walk where even he had been surprised at what they saw there: Elbert Fitz's ward and niece, half dressed and writhing in apparent ecstasy beneath Mr. Planck. As soon as they were discovered, the two of them had scrambled to their feet. Julie had taken a ring from her finger, thrown it down, and ground it into the dirt with her foot before running away, her shoulders and arms and half of her bosom exposed and half of the *ton* staring after her. She'd been utterly ruined.

And he'd stood there laughing.

It was the only time he saw her before their wedding day. How he'd laughed along with Elbert Fitz and Mr. Planck when Mrs. Drummond-Burrell had left in a glow with news to spread! How he'd laughed to himself when Mrs. Robertson sought him as husband for the girl years later!

But he wasn't laughing now.

He could walk in there and stop all of it. He could declare he was George DeMoray, and Julie would not have to sign away what was left of her fortune.

But then, as soon as Fitz and Planck returned to London, they would strip Chris's new identity from him. He would irrevocably be George DeMoray once more, and he'd be hauled away to debtors' prison if Sir Basil or Griselda or the Robertsons didn't take pity on him and lend him money enough to stave off his creditors. Chris didn't know which would be worse.

But it wasn't the indignity of prison or of taking a loan he dreaded. No, it was the look in Julie's eyes as she learned he was George DeMoray, the blackest of blackguards.

Could she forgive him? Would she see he was no longer George DeMoray, but Chris Christopher? Would she see he'd changed?

It wouldn't matter, he realized, for even if she forgave him, they could not be together. George DeMoray wouldn't have thought twice before accepting a loan from Basil and Griselda or signing the Countess of Westfold's paper, but the old George was gone. Chris Christopher would not accept a loan, and he would be imprisoned.

"She never has to know," he breathed. He could turn and walk away from Alderley and start a new life elsewhere. He deserved a new life. He *had* changed. He didn't know why or how the change had occurred, but he wasn't the same, and he knew he should not have to live with the old Whitemount's mistakes.

Silently he watched as Julie dipped her quill into the ink and signed the document. Griselda and Basil served as witnesses, Griselda weeping silent, angry tears and Basil's chin quivering. Julie set about blotting and drying the ink, and Chris took a last look inside before dropping his eyes and turning away and striding off into the darkness.

But he'd taken no more than twenty paces before he stopped.

He couldn't leave and start over, for the very reason that he *wasn't* the same man he had been. The old Whitemount would have walked away, but the new Whitemount would not.

Determined and grim, he turned and walked to the steps. Inside, three Robertson footmen— tonight's watch—stood listening at the library door.

"Mr. Christopher!" one hissed as he approached. "There are some curious odd culls in there, sir, and we don't like them at all."

"I will take care of this," George said. "Go back to your posts." *The fewer witnesses, the better.*

The three threw each other worried glances, but they followed his orders and retreated, and George pulled open the library doors.

Twenty-one

"Christopher!" In spite of her situation, Julie's face lit up, and she hurried to his side. "Oh, Christopher, I am so glad to see you. Where have you been? Sir Basil and Lady Griselda would tell me nothing but that you'd gone to London. Did your memories return?"

"They did," he told her.

Her eyes grew round, and she swallowed. "Who are you?"

"Your husband," he said. "I am your husband."

Her eyes filled with tears. "Oh, Christopher, how gallant," she said on a sigh, misunderstanding completely. "It is no use. These men know who I married." She clearly thought he'd lied in order to rescue her.

But Fitz and Planck had taken his meaning correctly. They stared at him, taking in his changed appearance, realization dawning upon them that he was indeed the Viscount Whitemount.

"*Christopher?*" Elbert Fitz said, incredulous.

Julie faced her uncle. "This is Mr. Christopher Christopher, our butler. He is also the man I love, the choice of my heart." She turned back to George, her eyes shining. "I am free. My husband, George DeMoray, the Viscount Whitemount, is dead. We can marry as soon as the banns are called."

Behind her, Elbert Fitz and Howard Planck realized their peril. If this was George DeMoray, Julie needn't have signed that paper at all, for they could not claim to have seen him die. And if Whitemount had been here at Alderley since his disappearance, then they could not claim Julie was a bigamist without incriminating Planck with the same crime.

"The paper!" Elbert Fitz shouted and Planck snatched the thing from the table as Fitz grabbed a poker from beside the fireplace.

But George was ready for them. For ten minutes, his muscles had been bunched, his whole being tightly coiled and ready to spring. Grabbing two alabaster shepherdesses from a table just next to him, he threw them hard, one at each man, deliberately not pausing long enough to achieve any sort of accuracy. It worked. Planck ducked his head and hesitated just long enough for George to advance and swing. His fist made swift, crushing, perfectly accurate contact with the man's nose, and down Mr. Planck went, down to the accompaniment of the sound of bells ringing.

Bells?

George spun to take care of Fitz, only to find the job half-done. Griselda and Julie were pelting him with a shower of heavy silver bells from the mantel, neither of them throwing like little girls but rather like Pictish warriors. The poker flailed ineffectually in the air as the man attempted to defend himself—to no avail. Coming up behind him, George gripped the poker with both hands, brought it down, and pulled it hard against Elbert Fitz's throat. Fitz grasped wildly at the poker, but George had the advantage of leverage, and Fitz could not shake him. George was ready for the arm that inevitably darted up, seeking George's eyes, hair—any vulnerability. Dropping the poker, he grasped the arm, and in one smooth motion that belied its savage nature, twisted it behind Fitz's back, simultaneously bending the hand at the wrist almost to the point of breaking.

Fitz gave a howl of pain and stilled instantly. "Please," he begged. "Please, do not break it!"

"I ought to," George said on a growl. "It is much less than you deserve. I ought to kill you for what you have done to Julie. And if you ever come near her again, I *will* kill you."

With one arm locked around Fitz's shoulder and the other around his wrist, George pulled the faked marriage certificate from the man's coat pocket and then propelled him toward the door, only then noticing several sets of eyes peering into the library. The clanging of the bells had brought the watch running and had awakened several others. Their expressions were filled with respect for Mr. Christopher's heroics.

Mr. Christopher. George looked away and swore.

Pushing Julie's uncle past the servants and down the steps, he called to one of the servants to hold the men's horses until he had revived Mr. Planck with a flower vase full of water and then treated him to the same sort of escort outside.

"If either of you ever speak one word to my wife, contact her, or bother her in any way, if I ever see anything but your retreating backs within her sight, or if you threaten anyone else here at Alderley, I will use this"—he waved the marriage certificate—"and the other paper you brought here to see you transported—if you are lucky. Be gone!" he commanded the two, nodding to a footman to toss the riders their reins.

A look of pure hatred flared in Elbert Fitz's eyes

before it was extinguished by his utter defeat. Off the pair rode into the night, never to be seen again.

More servants and the Robertsons had joined the throng, and the entry hall behind George was a sea of sleepy, curious expressions of people all clamoring for an explanation for the strange goings-on. But George did not heed them, for when he turned, there was only one face he saw, one voice he heard.

Julie was standing alone in the library doorway at the far end of the cavernous room. Her mouth moved, and, though his ears couldn't possibly have heard her over the cacophony, his heart heard her perfectly.

"Your wife?" she whispered. "Your wife?"

He nodded, hope and fear blending and building to a fevered crescendo that started the earth shaking beneath him. He waited for what seemed like hours as full realization dawned in her eyes, and she put together the broken pieces of these past days, the past five years, the broken pieces of her life. All the pieces were there now. Together, the two of them would assemble the pieces into a whole. He waited for her to realize, as had their old friends, that he had changed, that he wasn't the man she married, that he'd been reborn.

With shaking fingers, he unwound the bandage covering his burned hand. The injury had withered to a blackened scar. "My memory was restored to me in London." Pulling forth from his pocket her necklace and holding it out to her, he showed her his palm.

"Look at my scar," he said. "When the lightning struck, I was holding your locket. It branded me, as sure as loving you has branded my very soul.

Both marks will always be with me." The golden chain dangled from his fingers, an offering of his heart. *Take it,* he willed her. *Take it.* "You love me," he whispered.

"No," she said. "I loved Mr. Christopher, a man who never existed. I have never loved you, and I never will. You hid that scar as you hid your identity. You have been lying all along, attempting to seduce the other half of my fortune away from me."

She was wrong, of course. He hadn't ever lied to her, and he hadn't been after her fortune, but George was all too aware that, only a few minutes before, he had *intended* to lie to her and to keep lying to her for the rest of his life. If not for her uncle, George would have pretended to be Chris Christopher forever more. He had thought he'd changed, but now he wasn't sure. Was he reverting to his old personality? What sort of man was he now?

What sort of man was willing to base his marriage— and his entire life—on a lie?

As though she could hear his thoughts, she said, "You have not changed one whit, and you never will." Turning then, she left him for the last time, only this time she did not run. This time, her decision was not driven by fear and pain and a desire to hide, but by reason and consideration. She would not forgive him, and she did not want him.

The hall had quieted. Though none but Basil, Griselda, and the Robertsons understood exactly what had just occurred, they could see plain enough that their Miss Julie had just rejected their Mr. Christopher.

"Aw, she'll come around, sir."

"There, there."

"Poor boy."

"Lovers' quarrels, sir—they're soon mended."

"I'm that sorry, Mr. Christopher."

George read compassion and concern in the faces around him. Not once in London had he elicited such a reaction. How would these people react when they discovered who he really was and all that he'd done?

He'd been wrong to think he could just walk away and leave his old life behind. He couldn't escape who he was. His past was a part of him.

But his old ways didn't have to be.

The old Whitemount would have walked away from Julie's plight and started a new life, but the new Whitemount had not. Likewise, the new Whitemount would take responsibility for his actions—and for his past actions as well.

Everyone was staring at him. "Well. . . ." he said and solemnly shook Mr. Bendleson and John's hands, embraced Sir Basil, and kissed Griselda and Ophelia's foreheads. "I thank you all." He bowed and then he climbed the stairs.

"Where are you going?" Ophelia interjected into the silence behind him.

"To London," he said. "Where I belong."

Twenty-two

The morning came, fresh and beautiful. A soft breeze blew in the trees, and the sky was the deepest of cloudless blues. Chased by nightmares, Julie emerged into that pleasant day from the world of sleep and immediately wished she could escape into sleep once more. Bright reality was worse than the darkest of her dreams.

She shut her eyes tight.

"Good morning."

Julie gasped and turned toward the voice. There in the corner, watching her, sat a man. She sat up, jammed on her spectacles, and peered at him. "Sir Basil!" She took a more careful look and wrinkled her nose. "La, you look worse than I feel—like you have been sitting there all night."

"I have," he said. "I wanted to be here when you awoke."

Such a pronouncement by any other man would have been cause for alarm, but with Sir Basil, unusual behavior was quite usual, and, since he obviously thought nothing of being there, Julie tried to behave as though they were taking tea in the parlor rather than chatting alone in her bedchamber.

"Ah . . . lovely day is it not?"

"I suppose," he said.

"Umm . . . do you need something, sir?" she asked.

"I need to talk to you about Christopher."

"George DeMoray, you mean," she said, shaking her head and rubbing her neck.

"No, I mean Christopher—for so I will think of him to the end of my days."

"What about him?" she asked, her tone less than charitable.

"A good, sound name, is it not—Christopher? It is one of my second names, you know. Basil Christopher Blane Nairn."

"You will pardon me if I do not share your enthusiasm."

He looked at her then, not with the slightly rheumy and absentmindedly cheerful gaze she was used to, but with clear, steady, piercing eyes burning bright with intelligence and awake on all suits.

"Years ago," he said, "when I sailed to America, I learned that in order to chart a ship's course, one must have knowledge of the bottom, the currents, the weather, the stars, the ship, the crew—and if one is missing any of that information, the ship may run aground. It is important to have complete—oh, hell and blast! What I am trying to say is that, as you are Christopher's wife, I feel there are certain facts you should know about him—and about me."

"You, sir?"

"Indeed." He shifted uneasily in his chair and after a few moments said, "His mother loved the name Christopher, but she could not name the boy that, of course. There would have been talk. There was enough talk as it was."

Julie gave him a sidelong look. "What are you saying?"

He sighed heavily. "She was young and beautiful, and I was nearly fifty—not that it mattered, for I was in love with her, you see. Genuinely in love, and she with me. Mine was the first claim on her heart, but the Earl of Westfold's title and fortune, greater than my own, claimed her father's heart. She married him, and I left for the continent to lick my wounds." He shook his head at the memory. "When I returned eight months later, she had just given birth to her only son."

He smiled sadly. "We had kept our *tendre* secret, and for the first four years of his life, I was a frequent visitor to Westfold Hall. I do not know if he is mine, and neither did my dear Martha, but he could be, and I have watched over him his entire life. It was a promise I made to Martha as she lay in her bed dying—while her husband lay in his lover's bed."

His face filled with thunder then, and Julie thought he was finished, But as the seconds ticked by, his expression subsided, and he leaned back wearily into his chair.

"I am content," he said. "Please understand, I love Griselda just as dearly as I loved my fair Martha. When Sir Matthew Charles pulled that medallion from the cake,"—he shook his head—"I wanted to die."

He lapsed into silence again and stared out the window at the blue sky, absently running his hands over the mahogany arms of the chair. Julie remained silent, sensing there was more to his tale, and she was right. After a few moments, Basil lifted his gaze.

"Martha died, and I mourned—too much. Westfold noticed and gave me the cut. I do not know if he suspected his son was mine, but I was no longer welcome at Westfold Hall, and I had to content myself with keeping watch from afar." He made a fist, remembering. "Westfold is a hard man, and his lover soon came to regret having married him. The new Lady Westfold is a vain and selfish woman—and a barren one, as fate would have it. Westfold blamed her for it, accused her publicly of taking measures to avoid being with child. They quarreled bitterly and separated within two years.

"The boy was left in the country, alone and forgotten.

"The servants were no kinder than their masters in that house, and Christopher was frightened, angry, and sour. The servants turned him out during the day. He had a habit of wandering the lanes, and I encountered him there a few times, in the years before he was sent away to school.

"I would stay in a nearby village and discover what I could about him there. He was a thoroughly unpleasant lad, and quite understandably disliked by most everyone I met. I suspect he wouldn't have had anything to do with me but for the ladies—I have always kept dogs, you see—but Christopher loved animals. He was not gentle with me, but he was gentle with the ladies, and I loved watching him with them, for then I knew goodness had not been entirely driven from him.

"Still, I could do nothing but watch. Any further chance of seeing him ended when he was sent away to school, Eton and then university, and when he came away from Oxford, he rose to the top of society in a desperate attempt to find someone to love him—not that he recognized it for what it was, but I did, and my heart ached—especially when he was thrown down so violently. He spiraled down with the blue devils and into desolation. Frankly, my dear, I worried he might take his own life. That is why I was following him that night.

"And then he was struck by lightning and lost his memory, and I saw it for the miracle it was, a chance for him to start over, to be reborn, and I was right, he *was* reborn. He grew like a flower in the sunshine here. How it warmed my heart to see him—especially with you! I did not know he had married, you see. He managed to keep that secret even from me."

He stood and, walking to the window, hands clasped behind his back, stared out upon the morning and sighed. "It was almost like seeing him as a boy, watching him laugh and romp with my ladies once more."

Sir Basil turned and smiled, clearly remembering those early days. Julie could not help picturing Christopher as a boy, romping over a meadow with a pack of dogs.

"He has always loved dogs," she said. "He said he remembers being very small and having friends of his parents come to the estate with their dogs."

Basil grinned. "Bless me, but that was probably my ladies!" He chuckled, clearly pleased, but then his face slowly folded into lines of concern once more. "Do you know . . . I found Lady Cowper under a bridge. She was cold and wet, and she was so starved she could not move another step. I took her in, of course, but as I lifted her into my arms, she attempted to bite me. She tried to bite me every time I fed her, but I understood why, for she flinched each time I moved my hand, and she was covered with scars. Her poor ribs were knobby with old breaks. It was obvious the poor thing had never known any kindness." He chuckled softly again and then stood up straight and tall, his blue eyes piercing hers. "A year later, she was a perfect lady." He touched his hand to his mouth.

"Which reminds me, I must check on her and the pups. Good day!"

He quit the room suddenly, and Julie stared after him, quivering.

His message was clear. Christopher was like Lady Cowper, in a way.

Julie wandered to the window and looked out upon the distant meadow, where they'd sat upon the rock. "He lost his mother and his father at once," she murmured. "He was abandoned."

With his father remarrying and leaving him in the country with cruel servants, he'd had every reason to be angry and afraid. And when children were angry and afraid, they lashed out. Julie could imagine how it had been. The less compassion the servants had shown him, the worse he'd behaved, and the worse he'd behaved, the less compassion they'd shown him. There had been no escape.

She sighed and pushed up her spectacles to pinch the bridge of her nose.

"He may not be the good and noble man you thought you'd fallen in love with," she told her reflection on the windowpane, "but neither is he the frightened, angry child he was, nor the empty, cruel man he grew to be."

Sir Basil was right. George DeMoray *had* changed. But had he changed enough?

She turned away from the window and got out of yesterday's clothes. He was downstairs somewhere, and she'd have to face him sooner or later—either that or find another position, which was unthinkable. Alderley Manor was home, and those who lived there family.

She washed and pulled her brown calico over her head. Was it possible she'd been wrong about him?

Was it possible he truly hadn't regained his memory before London, that he wasn't merely pretending to care for her in order to take her remaining fortune?

By the time she was fully dressed and checked her image in the mirror, she could see her pulse beating rapidly at her neck.

"Calm . . . steady . . ." she told her reflection. Her eyes were too bright, her color too high. But she couldn't help it.

Perhaps she'd been wrong,—about part of it.

Perhaps he truly had fallen in love with her.

As she descended the stairs, she willed her heart to slow. It was going to take time to be certain. Only with time could she be sure her husband—her *husband!*—loved her.

Her heart clattered in her chest as she walked into the kitchen, half-expecting to see him there. But there was only one figure in the kitchen, Cook. She was standing at the far end with her back to Julie.

"Good morning, Cook," Julie said, wondering what the Robertson servants were off doing. "Where is everyone?"

"London," Cook said, not turning around. Julie thought she heard a sniffle. "They left this morn, early," Cook said. She wiped at her face and sniffled again.

Julie dashed to her side. "Cook, whatever is the matter?"

"Oh, Miss Julie . . . they are all gone, and it's all over, and her ladyship's wed to Sir Basil, and I know I should be happy about that, and I am—truly I am!—but things are going to be lonely around here, just the same, and I—I've been a watering pot all morning!"

"Aww . . . poor Cook," Julie said, putting her arms

around her friend. "I am certain things will be more lively here from now on. How can they not be with Sir Basil about?" She smiled, but Cook would have none of it.

"I need help," she said. "I got used to it, miss, and that's a fact. I just don't know what I shall do without those Robertson servants—to say nothing of Mr. Christopher, begging your pardon, miss. I know you two have your differences, but it seems to me you could work them out." She gave Julie an accusatory look. "Do you think you will?" she asked hopefully. "London ain't that far away."

Julie stood motionless. "Do you mean he is gone?"

Cook nodded. "Did you not know, miss? He left last night. Just walked off into the dark with nothing but the clothes on his back. He didn't even take Doctor Brown's horse. Which reminds me—" She bustled over to the dish shelf. "He left this for the good doctor, and this"—she pulled down Julie's teacup—"for you." She held out a folded sheet of paper with *Doctor Brown* written on the front and tipped the cup forward so Julie could see inside.

There, inside the cup, lay her locket.

"Now, everyone's been talking, and we're all sure what you be thinkin,' but he wouldn't even take so much as a morsel of food with him, miss, and he left your locket. That don't sound like a man bent on getting his hands on your fortune to me—and neither did the contents of that note."

"You read it?"

"Bless me, why wouldn't I? My pet had his poor heart broken and left with nothing. Of course I read it! And you ought to, too." She pushed the note into Julie's hands.

"Thank you, Cook." Julie took the note and the

locket and went out into the garden to sit on the bench, her hands shaking.

The morning sun had almost dried away the dew. The birds sang in the trees and blue butterflies danced in the flowers, but she could take no joy from the beauty of the day. He was gone, and she no longer had the luxury of time. She would never know if she'd been wrong about him. She'd never know if he'd truly loved her.

I am a messenger, he'd said, *brought here to remind Miss Julie Williams that time is fleeting.*

How right he'd been!

Twenty-three

The King's Bench wasn't a horrible prison, as prisons went. It was a debtor's prison, mostly, and it was south of the River Thames, so the air was less smoky, if a little more damp than at the Fleet. There was little for the prisoners to do at the King's Bench but gamble away money they did not have, visit with family, and read, for the guards could be persuaded to lend books for a price.

But George had no family or friends to bring him a pittance, and so he had nothing to pay with. While other prisoners with no money whatsoever spent time staring longingly through the gate or through their barred windows toward home and hearth, he spent all of his time in his cell.

A pecking order existed within the Bench's population, and George was near the bottom. His cell was small and had no window, but he didn't care, for there was nothing for him to look out upon. He had no home to long for, no one waiting for him on the outside. He spent his time in physical exercise, exhausting himself so that when he slept, his sleep would be dreamless.

Otherwise, he dreamt of her.

It was mid-September and late afternoon when he received his first visitor. *The Countess of Westfold,* he thought. He'd walked into the King's Bench voluntarily. It was unheard of, and he was sure the story had spread. He'd been expecting his stepmother's visit.

He washed carefully in his room and pasted on a nonchalant expression as he strode easily down the chill hall to a room near the warden's office. She stood at the far end, her back to him.

"What do you want?" he asked.

The woman turned at the sound of his voice, and shock coursed through him. This was not the countess.

"Hello, Christopher," Julie said.

After days of seeing nothing but the grays and browns of the King's Bench, the blue of her flowered calico gown and blue-green of her eyes made him blink against their brilliance. He swallowed and turned away from her, though it would have been easier to cut off his own hand. He could not allow her to see how much the sight of her affected him.

"What are you doing here?" he asked.

"I could ask you the same."

"I am taking responsibility for my actions. I have debts, and if I have to sit here in the King's Bench until my father dies to settle them, then that is what I will do."

"I am sure your father would settle your debts, if you would allow him to."

He scoffed. "I have no doubt my father takes great pleasure in looking across the Thames and knowing I am here."

"You are wrong. Your father mourns your loss."

He whirled around. "You have seen him?"

She nodded. "I see him every day. Oh, Christopher," she said, "did you never wonder why it was that Basil was the one to rescue you?"

He gave her a hard stare. "What are you saying?"

"I am saying it was no coincidence he was nearby the night you were struck by lightning. He was following you, watching over you as he had all your life. He had made a promise to your mother, you see, but he could not be with you always. He has suffered because he could not protect you, could not stop the earl and your stepmother from pushing you aside."

George's heart thudded inside his chest. "Are you saying Sir Basil is . . ."

"Do you remember telling me of the visitors' dogs when you were a small boy? Sir Basil has always kept dogs."

George pulled out a hard chair from the table and sank into it, unsure his legs would hold him. "Sir Basil . . . my father?" He looked up wonderingly at Julie, who nodded, the ghost of a wistful smile on her face.

"He told me so himself," she said. "He came to me the morning after you left and said there were some things I needed to know."

"What else did he tell you?" he asked.

"Not much, a little of your childhood, that is all— but it was enough."

"Enough?" George asked. "Enough for what?"

She came to him then and, kneeling before him, took his hands in hers. Her white skin was almost unbearably soft, the sweet scent of lilac enveloped him, and George had to fight to keep himself from pulling her onto his lap and burying his face in her honey-colored hair.

"Enough for me to realize what happened to you at Alderley," she answered. "Oh, Christopher, you knew no kindness as a lad, and so you never learned to be kind yourself. You lashed out, which only made people treat you worse. Do you not see it yourself? It was an ever-increasing circle of hostility and isolation, a great void in your life that could have been filled if only someone had shown you kindness.

"And then someone did—at Alderley.

"When your past life was taken from you, you were free to be who you truly are inside. You responded naturally to the kindness shown you. You were kind in return, and everyone there misses you."

He turned his head away from her. "Not for long. I was there but a short time. They will forget."

She touched his shoulder. "No. They are all hoping you will return. Lady Cowper paces from window to window endlessly. Cook has made so many pots of eel soup that no one at Alderley will eat it and we must give it away. The Bloom children ask for you every time someone passes their farm, and your dishes are still sitting upon the shelf in the kitchen."

"They do not know who I really am."

She shook her head again. "They know. The Robertson servants know all there is to know about the *ton*, it seems. Everyone knows the full story now. It is all any of them talk about. They know exactly who you are—and so do I."

She pulled from her reticule a piece of paper— the note he'd written to Doctor Brown. "I read it," she admitted with no apparent remorse. *"Dear Doctor Brown,* she quoted, never taking her eyes from George's, *I owe you fourteen guineas plus interest, and I will pay as soon as I am able. I beg you to watch over Julie for me and to keep her safe, and I remain yours in sincere friendship, George DeMoray."*

She put one hand over her locket. "I accused you of attempting to seduce me, of attempting to lay hands upon my remaining fortune, but I know now I was wrong. You left Alderley with nothing and came here to take responsibility for your past actions. You are good inside, and you always were. It was the blackguard part of you that was false—and you have cast that aside.

"Oh, Christopher, you helped me find the strength to cast aside a part of myself as well."

She stood and reached once more into her reticule. Pulling forth a sheaf of papers, she handed them to George. "Your vowels," she said simply, "all of them. I paid every one of your creditors."

"I owed a fortune," he said, in awe.

"Half a fortune, actually." She flashed him a brief smile, but it faded as quickly as it had appeared. "I have nothing left, but I am content—and unafraid. I know you will pay me back when you are able. I trust you."

She turned to go, but George reached out and stopped her.

"You married George DeMoray, the Viscount Whitemount, a blackguard. Are you willing to marry this George?" He placed his hand over his heart. "A penniless dog watcher? An incompetent butler, who builds smoky fires and cuts candle wicks too short? A man who loves you?"

Her heart in her eyes, Julie walked slowly back to him. Stopping inches in front of him, she took his hand.

"I, Julie Fitz, do solemnly swear—"

"I, George Christopher Blane DeMoray do solemnly swear—"

"—to take thee, George, as my wedded husband . . ."

"—to take thee, Julie, as my wedded wife . . ."

The wedding ceremony was over with even more quickly this time than it was the first time, five long years before. There was no church, no veil, no flowers, no fancy carriage, no gown, not even a witness. But this time, there was a proper kiss. And when Julie and George left the makeshift wedding chapel, they left together and turned toward home.

The messages were given and received, and neither of them was ever alone again.

Epilogue

"Happy Christmas!" the cry sounded through the drawing room at sunset and was echoed over and over all evening.

Alderley Manor was the scene of another grand house party. It had begun as a simple affair, with Sir Basil and Lady Griselda inviting only the Robertsons, but Ophelia had suggested "a few additions" to the party, and the guest list had grown precipitously. Four other couples, three of them young and with children—ten in all, ranging from twelve to just one year—accepted, and, with the addition of the young and energetic new Alderley servants—Basil and Griselda's gift to everyone at Alderley Manor—the house was full to the rafters and merrier than it had ever been.

It was Christmas Eve, and a hundred beeswax candles—none with their wicks too short—filled the drawing room with the sweet smell of honey. Sir Basil and Griselda sat with the Robertsons and the dowager Countess of Lindenshire and her husband, Mr. Peabody, the six of them happily dandling children upon their knees as the children's parents worked to hang greenery or helped the older children manufacture kissing boughs. In the corner, the Earl of Lindenshire played carols upon his harp and

sang, his voice deep and clear. Two or three of the
children clustered around his knees, singing along.

Julie watched with a smile as Christopher—as he
would always be known here—sang right along.
He'd learned many carols and lullabies and games,
and he romped now with some of the younger children as he sang—playing *friendly singing horse.*

Sitting beside Julie, The Gypsy, Artemis Chase, the
Countess of Lindenshire, nudged her and nodded
in Christopher's direction. "The change in him is
amazing," she said.

It was The Gypsy whom the Viscount Whitemount
had tried to ruin, to his own utter downfall. It was
The Gypsy who had supplied the medallions to
Ophelia for Griselda's use, and no one was more
happy with the results than she. Julie quite liked her,
and she and Artemis had become fast friends.

"He will be a wonderful father," Artemis remarked.

Julie smiled and looked from her husband to
Artemis. "Yes. I think he will. And speaking of father-
hood,"—Julie reached out to brush her hand against
a small blue and white quilt Artemis was embellishing
with the most beautiful blue embroidery—"that looks
suspiciously like a baby-sized quilt. Will you be needing it any time soon?"

Lord and Lady Lindenshire already had a two-
year-old, a lovely little imp who was really Artemis's
little sister.

Artemis smiled and fingered a square of ornate
blue damask shot with silver that was worked into
the center of the quilt. "This little square has quite a
story behind it," she said, averring. "It has passed
from couple to couple." She inclined her head toward the others. "It began as Nigel's waistcoat and
passed to Marianna, who used it to trim a pair of

stockings, which I found on the side of the road. They were a sign that led me to wed my dear Orion. I made them into doll clothes for our Anna"—she smiled at her husband, who waved back with a boyish grin—"and now it is going into this quilt. It is a sign, a portent, a charm linking us all, a symbol of our friendship and goodwill."

"Can I assume you will be gifting your husband with a child this new year?" Julie tried again, leaning over to finger the square of damask.

"No," Artemis said with a smile, "but you will."

Julie's mouth dropped open. "How do you know that? We have not told a soul."

Artemis only laughed and kept on working.

Julie wandered over to Christopher and gave him a hug. Ostensibly, he was still the Alderley butler, though with the addition of the new servants, he was free to do nothing but supervise the staff—which was fortunate, since Julie hadn't the time for it anymore. Doctor Brown had moved to Buxley-on-Isis a month before. He spent half of his time there anyway, he said, and Julie had become as competent a physician as he. She was officially taking care of the villagers and those at Alderley now, and she was happier than she'd ever thought possible.

"I am glad you did not accept the invitation to Brighton Pavilion for Christmas," she told Christopher. "Who else could build a fire that fine?" She nodded toward the Yule log burning upon the hearth.

His palm brushed over her belly and he looked into her eyes. "Thank you," he said, "for everything."

In the corner, Ophelia Robertson looked upon them all—at the six couples she had brought together, at the children capering about the room with the puppies Sir Basil had given each young family. The world outside was filled with the soft hush of a deep snowfall. The drawing room was filled with adult laughter and song, with the pop and hiss of the fire, and with the excited shrieks and giggles of children, and Ophelia was filled with contentment. Her work was done.

ABOUT THE AUTHOR

Melynda Beth Skinner lives in Florida, with her husband and their charming hellions, two lovely little girls who make their mama and papa very proud. She enjoys hearing from readers. You may write to her at: 7259 Aloma Avenue, Suite 2 Box 31, Winter Park, FL 32792. Please enclose SASE if you wish a reply. Or visit her at *www.melyndabethskinner.com*, where you can send her an e-mail or chat with her online.

If you liked this story, you may also enjoy the first three novels. *The Blue Devil, Miss Grantham's One True Sin,* and *Lord Logic and the Wedding Wish,* are intertwined with *The Blackguard's Bride* in some surprising ways—including appearances by the outrageous and clever Ophelia Robertson.

Complete Your Collection Today
Janelle Taylor